CW01090923

# TWISTED

# FAMILIAR

## L.M. HATCHELL

Twisted Familiar

The Pussy Chronicles (Book 1)

Cover Design by Real Life Design Covers

Editing by Two Birds Author Services

Copyright © 2024 by L.M. Hatchell

All rights reserved. No part of this publication may be reproduced, stored or transmitted in any form or by any means, electronic, mechanical, photocopying, recording, scanning, or otherwise without written permission from the publisher. It is illegal to copy this book, post it to a website, or distribute it by any other means without permission.

This novel is entirely a work of fiction. The names, characters and incidents portrayed in it are the work of the author's imagination. Any resemblance to actual persons, living or dead, events or localities is entirely coincidental.

# FOREWORD

My editor and I have made every effort possible to catch all typos, but we're human and those things can be sneaky buggers. If you come across any errors, please drop me a message at author@lmhatchell.com and I'll make sure they get dealt with (yep, those are meant to be s's not z's ;).

I love hearing from readers so don't hesitate to reach out and let me know what you think of the book!

# CHAPTER ONE

Thirteen pairs of golden eyes stared down at Jem, as hard and unyielding as the granite dais the cats sat on. The weight of their combined judgement pinned him in place like he was the mouse he'd been toying with that very morning, and he shifted uneasily.

"You blew up her potions room."

The accusation came from the short-haired black cat perched on a cream and gold cushion at the far left of the thirteen. Sir Rogers III, Thirteenth Elder of the Feline Familiar Society, and snooty twat with an irritatingly pompous voice. Jeremiah Snufflekins – or Jem, as he was known to those who didn't have their head so far up their own arses that their whiskers tickled their intestines – detested the cat, and often imagined leaving a nasty surprise in his tuna.

Trying to look suitably repentant, Jem cleared his

throat. "I wouldn't say that *I* blew up her potions room. The flammable potion she left lying around did that."

A pregnant silence filled the large, circular chamber that held court to disciplinary proceedings for the FFS. Jem cringed despite himself.

This whole thing was so unfair. If the witch hadn't withheld the catnip, he wouldn't have gone on a midnight zoom around the house. He needed the damn catnip to help him sleep, so really it was her own fault that he knocked over the potion and caused the room to explode.

Anyway, it was only a minor explosion. One room. It hardly singed her nose hairs. And they'd wiped the next-door neighbour's memory, so no harm done really. Unless, of course, you counted the old man forgetting to put clothes on when he left the house the next day, but Jem could hardly be held responsible for that little side effect. As usual, FFS were making a fuss about nothing.

"This is the eighth time you've been returned to us by a witch charge we've assigned to you," Sir Rogers continued, not even acknowledging Jem's defence. "Eight times you've faced the disciplinary panel."

*Lucky me.*

Jem only just managed to restrain himself from sticking out his tongue at the cat. It wasn't his fault that all the witches he'd been assigned to were too soft.

Come on, so what if he'd gotten one fired from her day job? He'd told her it was a bad idea to bring him to the office, but apparently she didn't think he could be trusted at home. And the one who burned off her hair and eyebrows after mixing up his spell instructions – which might or might not have been a little hazy – looked better bald anyway.

The ones who complained about the noise he made while playing at three o'clock in the morning were the worst. Why should he have to stick to their schedule? He'd kept his claws retracted when he pounced on them. What more did they want?

"What say you?" demanded Magdalena, from her position at the centre of the thirteen.

He blinked. Oh, they'd been expecting a response? Would they actually bother listening even if he gave one?

Jem swished his tail, his eye catching on a tassel that swung from the corner of Magdalena's gold cushion. "Eh, not guilty?" he mumbled, distracted by the movement.

Back and forth. Back and forth. He itched to take a swipe at it.

A disappointed sigh snapped him out of his tassel trance, and he looked up at the eyes that were as familiar as his own cerulean ones. There was a sadness in Magdalena's expression that almost made him feel guilty. Almost.

She'd never been much of a mother to him. Her role as First Elder demanded all her attention, and it was clear that being a mother meant little to her. She popped out the kittens as if it was her duty to ensure the continued survival of the familiar population, but raising them was a different story altogether.

Still, it was hard to shake the innate desire to please her, even if decades had passed since he was that naïve kitten longing for a mother's affection.

"I cannot protect you any longer, Jeremiah." She gave a resigned shake of her head. "Our cause here is too great, and your actions put our world in danger of being once again exposed to humans. I cannot allow it to continue."

At her words, Zachariah, the Elder to her right, stepped down from his gold gilded cushion. He padded to a scroll resting on the floor of the dais and swatted it with a paw, unrolling it.

"Jeremiah Snufflekins," he said, in a voice so monotonous it would've made Jem nod off if it wasn't for the adrenaline holding him rigid before the Elders. "You are being charged with your eighth misdemeanour in your capacity as a witch familiar. It is hereby decreed that you are on your final life. The Elders have conferred and the decision is unanimous. You will be assigned to a rehabilitation trainer for a period of one month. During this time, you will be required to pass a series of inspections. If you do not pass, we will have no choice but to strip you of your powers. For good."

*What?*

Was that even possible? He was a familiar. They couldn't take away his magic. Could they? A chilling cold washed through him, and he shook his head in disbelief.

As if reading his thoughts, his mother said quietly, a tinge of regret edging her tone, "We can, and we will do it, Jeremiah. You've given us no choice."

This was a joke. It had to be. They were going to send him to another trainer? Another witch like her... Nausea twisted his insides at the thought.

"There's really no need for this," he insisted, panic rising in him. "Just assign me another charge. I'll be on my best behaviour."

"You've had your chances," Sir Rogers sneered, looking down his nose at Jem. "Eight of them."

"It has been decided, and so it shall be," Magdalena declared, all compassion gone from her voice.

With that, the thirteen Elders relaxed down onto their respective cushions in a clear sign of dismissal. Oblivious to, or uncaring of, the inner monologue of furious denial that was running through his head, some set about grooming themselves while others lapped at the bowls of water placed in front of them by the human witch aides.

Jem stared at them in disbelief. That was it? They were seriously going to do this to him, then go about their business as if nothing had happened?

Could a familiar even survive without their magic? He'd only ever heard rumours about familiars having their magic stripped...

It was who he was; being a familiar was all he'd ever known. They effectively assigning him a death sentence, and they hadn't even once stopped to consider the possibility that he wasn't the problem. Maybe some witches weren't cut out for a familiar – did they ever think of that?

Well, screw them. He'd pass their stupid inspections, but if they expected him to be best buds with the trainer, they'd be sorely disappointed. He'd made that mistake once before. He wouldn't make it again.

Shoving away the lingering sense of dread, he turned on his tail and stalked from the chamber. As he moved through the winding corridors of the FFS headquarters, his anger grew. No doubt they'd already decided he was going to fail. Well, he'd show them. He'd be the best damn familiar they'd ever seen.

He held that thought with fierce determination as he scaled the climbing frame and emerged into the old library that concealed the entrance to the FFS HQ. Floor-to-ceiling bookcases loomed on either side of him, and he rubbed his body against the nearest one, purring as the musty scent of the books tickled his nose.

Oh, yes. He'd be on his best behaviour...

For now, at least.

CHAPTER TW⊙

The detached red brick house was nestled innocuously at the centre of a quaint housing estate. It looked about as far from a witch's house as the stories would have you believe – no yummy gingerbread decorations for him to snack on at all. Jem snickered as he thought of the clueless humans who no doubt thought their neighbour to be a nice, normal young lady.

As the stony-faced man at his side reached out to press the doorbell, Jem resigned himself to his fate. He'd been debating whether or not to indulge in more catnip when the witch aide had rudely interrupted him at the ungodly hour of noon that morning. The Elders apparently had doubts about his willingness to find his way to his new assignment and so had arranged an escort.

The door opened, and a young woman with bright purple hair looked down at him. She smiled, her blue eyes sparkling as she did. Jem stared blankly.

"Ms. Blackwood." The witch aide gave a respectful tilt of his head in greeting, but his hard expression didn't soften even a little.

"Richard. Good to see you again."

Jem couldn't be sure if it was his imagination, but he'd swear the sparkle in her eyes dimmed somewhat as she addressed the man. As a top-level trainer, she'd likely encountered many of the human FFS employees before. Did she find them as unbelievably tedious as he did, or did she snivel and pander to them just like all the other witches he'd encountered?

Oblivious or indifferent to the cool reception, Richard gave a dismissive wave towards where Jem stood at his feet. "Jeremiah Snufflekins. Your trainee."

Jem bristled, hissing his displeasure at the word.

The witch didn't seem to take his reaction personally, as some might have. Instead, she crouched down until she was almost at head height with him. Her gaze was assessing but friendly.

"I'm Melanie, but you can call me Mel. Would you like to come in?"

He plonked his arse down on the spot and sneered.

Mel's lips twitched in response, as if his show of defiance simply amused her. She straightened up and turned to make her way back into the house. "I'll leave the door open. You can join me whenever you're ready."

Jem watched her go, irritation bubbling up inside him.

Richard clearly didn't share the witch's patience, however. He nudged Jem with his obnoxiously shiny black shoe to get him moving.

Jem hissed again and swiped out with a paw. His claws connected with flesh, and though he only allowed himself to draw a little blood, it was enough to cause the man to swear. Satisfied, Jem stalked into the house, and with a swish of his tail slammed the door in Richard's face.

He found Mel at the end of the hallway in a bright, open kitchen. Teal coloured cabinets ran along one wall with a white marble-top island and tall stools in the centre. Bi-fold doors led to the outside and gave a view of the neatly landscaped garden beyond. An array of herbs formed perfect rows on one side of the grassy lawn, and vibrant flowers were in full bloom on the other, despite the fact it was almost winter.

Without waiting for her to acknowledge his presence, Jem jumped up on one of the high stools that surrounded the island where she sat. He waited for her to chastise him or issue a warning not to damage her furniture. Instead, she slid a plate of sushi over to him. His mouth watered.

Oh, he saw what she was at. Thought she could buy his cooperation, did she? Well, he'd show her.

He bit his tongue to stop himself from face-planting into the food and devouring it, and gave her the blank expression he'd perfected over many years of antagonising witches. Completely unfazed, she plucked a piece of sushi off her own plate with chopsticks and popped it into her mouth.

"Why don't we start by getting to know each other?" she suggested once she'd swallowed. "You could tell me a bit about yourself."

He stared at her.

She let the silence draw out, no doubt waiting to see if he'd crack. He would not.

Eventually, she sighed and crossed her arms. The shrewd intelligence in her eyes belied the bored expression she wore. "Let's not waste each other's time pretending you can't talk. I'm not a rookie. I earned my ability to speak to familiars over a decade ago. Do you really think you're the first to play mute?"

Jem blinked, his curiosity suddenly piqued. She didn't seem particularly old – mid-twenties at most. It was possible, of course, that the stupid purple hair just made her look more immature than her years. But if she'd developed the ability to speak with familiars over ten years ago, that would've made her a teenager. He could count on one paw how many witches had managed that. That was pretty impressive.

For most witches, it took until they were in their early twenties at least for them to come into their power sufficiently to communicate with a familiar. The familiar-witch relationship was a complex one, and a witch needed to first understand who they themselves were before they were equipped to appreciate it. Even for trainers – those who were particularly attuned to the magic of familiars – it was generally only once they turned eighteen, and were considered an adult within the magical community, that they developed the ability.

"You don't have a familiar of your own," he pointed out, somewhat snidely.

"True," she acknowledged. "I'm following a different path."

He bristled. Did she think she was too good for a familiar? Of course she did. All witches did. Never mind that a familiar's magic increased theirs tenfold if the bond was strong enough. These witches saw familiars as something to be used and discarded as they pleased. And the Elders wondered why he didn't want to be bonded to one.

Mel opened a luminous pink rucksack that rested on the floor next to her stool and tugged out an iPad. With a swipe, she unlocked it and scrolled to something he couldn't see on the screen.

"According to your file, you were inducted by one of the most respected trainers in the history of FFS. She gave you a glowing recommendation, so clearly skill level isn't the issue..."

Jem stilled at the mention of *her*. Mel was still talking through his documented list of strengths, but the white noise was growing so loud in his head that he could barely hear her words.

"...we'll concentrate on..."

He swiped a paw at the plate in front of him, causing it to rattle, and jumped down off the stool.

Mel stopped mid-sentence and looked at him in surprise.

"Where will I be sleeping?"

This time, it was her turn to blink. After a lengthy pause, she pushed the iPad aside and stood. No anger showed on her face at his rude interruption, but there was a noticeable shift in her demeanour as she beckoned him to follow her out of the kitchen.

"Come on. I'll show you to your room."

She led him upstairs without another word. He held his chin high as he walked, making it clear that this had been his idea and he wasn't obeying her orders by following.

Three doors lined the hallway at the top of the stairs. One stood open, revealing a grey and white tiled bathroom. Mel glanced back to make sure he'd taken note of it, the warning clear in her eyes: use it, or you'll be clearing up your own shit.

A tempting idea hula'd its way into Jem's mind, but he swatted it away reluctantly. Until these stupid inspections were out of the way, he had to at least make it seem like he was behaving. Passive-aggressive defiance was one thing. Leaving special presents in hard-to-find places was probably pushing his luck.

Mel continued past the second room and stopped at the final door at the end of the hallway. She pushed it open to reveal a small slice of kitty heaven.

Despite himself, Jem's tail twitched with barely restrained excitement.

One entire wall of the room had been turned into a climbing frame. Its winding pathways promised hours of entertainment, and the posts dotted at random intervals throughout just begged to be scratched. A large, plush cat bed rested in the corner covered in soft, grey blankets, and a wicker box rested on the floor next to it. The lid on the box was askew, allowing a tantalising glimpse of the assortment of toys contained within. Jem locked his muscles in place to stop himself from rushing in to bat at the thread of yarn hanging over the edge.

A stuffed rainbow-coloured bunny sat on top of the box and he tilted his head, eying it warily.

Noticing his attention, Mel smiled. "That's Mr. Fluffles. I'll leave you two to get acquainted. We start our training tomorrow."

Before he could respond with a snide remark about using it to sharpen his claws, she was gone, the door closing quietly behind her. Jem listened to her footsteps retreat down the stairs. Only when they'd faded entirely did he turn his attention back to the room.

It definitely wasn't the worst place he'd ever stayed. That honour went to the second-hand dog bed that had been missing half its stuffing and smelled of dog piss. In fact, given the bed looked suitably padded and a tentative sniff test suggested it was new and hadn't been used by another cat, this was possibly the best place he'd stayed. Maybe the witch wasn't all bad.

Before he could give the bed the requisite comfort test to decide exactly how high he'd rate her effort, there was something he needed to check.

The room was small enough that a single window allowed in ample light. It was split into two panes of glass with the top third forming a small window that could be opened. Easily large enough for a cat to fit through.

Careful to keep his movements silent lest the witch return to check on him, he leapt up onto the windowsill. He balanced on his hind legs and reached up to swat at the handle. It moved, and he nudged the window open.

A gentle breeze filtered in through the opening, and he stared at it thoughtfully. She hadn't locked him in. Did that mean he was free to come and go as he pleased? The Elders hadn't technically said he was under house arrest, but it seemed like quite a lot of freedom to allow a familiar that had been sent here for being a "troublemaker."

He'd think on it more later. Right now, he needed a nap.

Leaving the window ajar to allow in the fresh scent of the recent rain shower, he hopped down off the windowsill and padded over to the bed. A wary prod confirmed the bed wouldn't suddenly come alive and attack him, so he jumped up and set about making himself a comfortable groove.

He curled into a ball and wrapped his tail around himself, ready to welcome oblivion when his eyes fell on the stuffed bunny. He glared at it before stubbornly shutting his eyes. Then he opened them again.

With an irritated huff, he jumped up, swatted the bunny down off the box and dragged it back to the bed. He settled back into his groove, snuggled into Mr. Fluffles, and was asleep within minutes.

# CHAPTER THREE

The light had faded to a warm evening glow by the time Jem yawned and blinked one eye open. He stretched his paws out in front of him and arched back into a satisfying stretch. There was no sound that he could discern from the house so, curious, he leapt up onto the windowsill and peered out. The electric blue car that had been parked in the driveway on his arrival was gone. He eyed the empty spot in surprise.

Had she left him in the house alone? With his track record? Wow, this witch was either really naïve or was trying to test him.

He debated what kind of mischief he could get up to that would just toe the line rather than topple him head first over it. Top priority was to find out where the catnip was stored, since it was the only thing likely to make this whole experience bearable. First though, he needed to use the bathroom.

Jumping down off the windowsill, he took a moment to appreciate the soft, fluffy carpet beneath his paws. He made a mental note to roll on it later to test how soft it was, then padded to the door and nudged it open with his head.

The smell tickled his nose before his eyes registered the plate of sushi resting on the floor outside his room. He eyed it suspiciously, then poked it with his paw. Had the witch left it there?

Was this part of the test?

*First she leaves the window open so I can escape anytime I want. Then she leaves me home alone without even so much as a warning not to cause trouble. Now this?* It had to be a test.

Unable to help himself, he gave the plate a sniff. He couldn't detect any worrying odours beneath the mouth-watering smell of fresh tuna, and he hadn't yet annoyed Mel enough for her to want to poison him. Screw it!

He buried his face in the food like he'd wanted to do when she'd placed it in front of him in the kitchen. Within minutes, the plate was empty and he was a purring heap on the floor, full and contented. It was only with great effort that he managed to peel himself up to use the bathroom before making his way back to the room for a much-needed nap.

A knock on the door jolted him out of the blissful oblivion of sleep a few hours later. He blinked groggily, his left eye stuck stubbornly closed as daylight seared his right eye.

Wait. Was it morning?

Dammit! He'd only meant to have a quick nap after eating the sushi, not waste all that precious catnip hunting time. Bloody witch knew exactly what she was doing, distracting him with food. He'd have to be more on his guard with her.

Another knock sounded on the bedroom door.

"Jem?" Mel called. "It's time to start our training. I'll be waiting for you upstairs."

*Upstairs?* He hadn't noticed another stairway when Mel showed him to the room yesterday. Curiosity overrode his irritation and, begrudgingly, he climbed out of bed to go investigate.

Mel was nowhere to be seen when he opened the door. There was, however, a ladder extending from a hole in the ceiling. He padded to it and sniffed disdainfully. This was "upstairs"?

Huffing out a martyred sigh, he scaled the ladder in two agile bounds and was swallowed by the rectangular hole. There was a sense of pressure that caused his fur to stand on end. Then with a *pop*, the feeling was gone.

Jem found himself standing in a large, circular space. Skylights dotted the ceiling, directing beams of light into a prism at the centre of the room, and around that centre point, a pentagram shimmered on the floor. Each of the five points were filled with complex runes of protection and well-being. Their intricate design and clean, precise lines showed a skill he'd rarely seen before. Had Mel created the pentagram or paid another witch to do it?

Intrigued, he moved further into the space. Shelves ran along the left-hand side of the room, showcasing orderly rows of glass jars. White labels with neatly flowing handwriting denoted the contents, and he spotted various spell ingredients including sage, vervain, and mugwort.

The other side of the room was bare except for a long, wooden table. A pestle and mortar rested atop it next to a large, brown leather tome and several open jars. But it was the table itself that held Jem's attention.

Lovingly carved from the bark of an old oak tree, the table's surface showcased a rich history through the knots and grooves that mapped the tree's life in the wood. Energy permeated every inch of it, and while Mel wouldn't be able to harness that energy directly since she wasn't an elemental, it lent a sacred aura to the space that would strengthen any magical workings she completed here. It was breathtaking.

On the far side of the pentagram, Mel was making preparations for their training session. He knew without even asking what that training session would entail, and he was about as enthusiastic as a mouse about to be eaten by a cat. Witch-familiar bond, blah, blah, blah.

Finally acknowledging his presence, she clapped her hands and turned to him with a smile. "Shall we start by establishing a connection?"

*Ugh.* He had to fight down the urge to hack up a furball.

It was standard practice to complete a bonding ritual for a new witch-familiar pairing, though in truth, it wasn't necessary. A powerful familiar could easily augment a witch's magic without any kind of ceremony. One of his bloodline could do it in their sleep while dreaming of tuna if the witch was receptive enough. But witches did love their rituals, and many of them believed this kind of thing made them a "real" witch.

Not waiting for a response, Mel moved to the centre of the pentagram and collapsed cross-legged into a seated position on the ground. She looked at him expectantly.

Jem stared back just long enough to make it clear that when he finally stepped into the pentagram, it was by his own choice, not because she told him to. Her barely suppressed smile told him she thought otherwise, but what did she know.

"Now, I know from your previous assessments scores that you don't really need this," she said once he'd settled in place and given his balls a quick clean for good measure. "But I think it would be a good starting point for us to get a feel for each other's magic."

He gave her a bored look and she sighed.

Apparently taking his silence as a signal to proceed, she began the soft chant of the bonding ritual. As she spoke her power crackled around her, bright colours sparking and popping. Rarely had Jem seen colours so vibrant when connecting to a witch's magic, and once more he couldn't help but notice that her power level seemed unusually high given her young age.

When it came time to add his power to the ritual, he spoke the words in the most monotonous, irreverent tone he could manage, just in case it wasn't already clear to her that he was here under duress. Still, Mel gave him an encouraging smile.

Her energy sparked even brighter, and the miasma of colour reached out towards his own midnight blue aura, ready to join and become one. Right as the two were about to merge, Jem leapt out of the circle and away from the rainbow-like power that called to him.

Mel jerked back as if slapped. She looked at him in confusion, hurt flashing in her eyes.

He gave her his most innocent look, pushing away the twinge of guilt. "There was a mouse."

# CHAPTER FOUR

Mel was in a snit. She said she wasn't, but the clatter of pots and pans in the kitchen said otherwise.

He'd let her complete the bonding ritual on the third attempt when he'd gotten the sense that he was coming precariously close to pushing his luck. Now, the stupid bond tugged constantly at his centre, reminding him he was *tied* to a witch. He'd long stopped being that naïve young familiar who dreamed of the perfect witch pairing, and every time a bond was forced on him it made him feel like he was trapped, suffocating.

When even a snuggle with Mr. Fluffles didn't help his foul humour, he went in search of the one thing that would.

Prowling into the kitchen, he plonked himself right under Mel's feet and demanded, "Where's the catnip?"

She jumped back with a yelp, apparently too wrapped up in her preparations to have noticed his stealthy approach. "Dammit, Jem. I told you I need to get dinner ready before Derek arrives. Can your catnip addiction please wait until I'm done?"

He hissed and swiped at her with his paw. Who cared about her stupid boyfriend? He needed catnip.

With a sigh, she crouched down to his level. "I promise I'll get you catnip later. Please, just give me some space. Derek will be here in a few minutes." She stood back up and turned to open the fridge, burying her head inside as she rummaged about and muttered to herself.

He glared at her back. She wanted to keep the catnip from him, did she?

In one fluid motion he leapt up onto the kitchen counter, and with a swish of his tail, sent the jar of tomato sauce that rested there somersaulting into the air. It hit the floor with a satisfying smash.

"What the –" Mel jerked back out of the fridge and gaped in disbelief at the sauce now splattered all over the floor and the nearby cabinets.

That would show her!

Jem sashayed out of the kitchen and bounded up the stairs to his room, slamming the bedroom door behind him for good measure. Still angry, he scaled the climbing frame and found a spot at the top that was bathed in the late afternoon sun. He curled up into a ball and allowed the warmth on his fur to lull him into a fitful sleep.

The distant sound of voices awoke him a while later. He recognised the female voice as Mel's and could only assume the accompanying male voice to be the boyfriend. David? Dennis? Derek? Who cared!

Stretching back onto his haunches, he yawned. The daylight had faded to a pleasant reddish hue while he slept, and he guessed it must be early evening. He leapt down from his perch and contemplated the closed door and his options.

Would Mel stick to her promise to give him catnip after his little tantrum with the sauce? Yes, it had been petty of him, but the bonding ritual had made him cranky, and she'd refused to give him the one thing that might've helped him block it out. He could always see if she was in a better mood now that her boyfriend was here to make googly eyes at.

Cautiously, he opened the door and peered into the hallway.

Mel had warned him earlier that day that her boyfriend was human, and Jem either needed to make himself scarce for the evening or embrace his inner kitty. The magic world had very strict rules when it came to exposing the truth to non-magic users – the witch trials of the past had taught them all a hard-learned lesson. So, while it wasn't forbidden for a witch to date a human, it was under the strict proviso that any breaches of that rule would be swiftly and harshly punished.

In light of that, Jem would, of course, be on his best

familiar behaviour. That didn't mean he had to be on his best kitty behaviour, however.

Following the sounds of laughter, he padded down the stairs and crept on silent paws into the small, cosy living room. Two oversized turquoise sofas filled the space, set around an open fire that was currently blazing. From Jem's position in the doorway, he could see the back of Mel's head as she snuggled into a male who was every cliche of good-looking you could think of – tall, dark, handsome, with an athletic build that spoke of copious amounts of hours staring into a gym mirror. Jem immediately pegged him as a douche.

He listened for a moment as Derek recounted some snore-inducing tale from his day and wondered if he'd greatly overestimated Mel's intelligence. Surely she couldn't be taking this guy seriously?

At risk of dying of boredom simply by being in the same room as the two lovebirds, Jem decided the evening needed some added excitement. He eyed Mel and Derek's positions for the best angle, then tensing his hind legs, he propelled himself upwards.

With a leap worthy of the Olympics, he cleared the top of the sofa and landed squarely on the boyfriend's head.

Derek's screech was surprisingly high pitched as he jumped around the room swatting at his head in a panic. Of course, Jem had already jumped down to make himself comfortable on the recently vacated spot on the sofa, so the man was simply slapping himself.

"Jem!" Mel's exclaim was edged with barely contained fury as she hurried to calm her boyfriend.

He gave her his most innocent kitty look but struggled to keep his smirk from showing as she rubbed the boyfriend's arm in reassurance, her face red with embarrassment.

"I'm so sorry. I got a new foster cat and he's not quite house-trained yet." She darted another glare in Jem's direction.

The overly bright smile was back on Derek's face in an instant as he smoothed his shirt and surreptitiously checked to make sure each strand of hair was still in place. "Nothing to be sorry about." He waved away her apology. "I love cats."

Jem's hackles rose at the obvious lie, and he bared his teeth.

Derek moved to sit back down, but flinched when he saw his spot was now occupied. A flash of irritation caused his perfect mask to slip for a moment before he once more schooled his expression and lowered himself to the next cushion over with a smile. As if to highlight how sincere he was about his love of cats, he reached over and patted Jem's front paw.

Jem hissed, his claws unsheathing.

"I think I hear the oven beeping," Mel said, quickly jumping between the two of them, a nervous edge to her smile. "Maybe you should come with me while I take the dinner out, Jem? I can get you some yummy cat treats."

"Reow."

She glared daggers at him as he failed to budge even an inch. The irritating beeping continued in the background, and it was clear that she was torn between the primal need to save the dinner she'd slaved over and the worry of leaving him alone with Derek.

To assist in her decision-making, Jem wriggled about on the sofa to make a more comfortable groove for himself.

Eventually, the incessant beeping won out, and with a frustrated huff, Mel stalked from the room.

Jem waited until she was fully out of sight before turning his attention to the boyfriend, who still had that too-white smile on his face. Then he proceeded with the very important task of cleaning his balls.

A second later, he found himself tumbling through the air.

"Get out of my seat, you mangey fleabag," Derek snarled, the faux nice guy act dropped in a blink.

Jem jumped to his feet, arched his back, and hissed. How dare that human push him!

"What are you looking at?" Derek lashed out with his foot, forcing Jem to leap back to avoid being struck. "Bloody foster cats? What a load of bleeding heart shite. I'll have to see that she puts an end to that."

As Derek plonked himself back in his earlier spot on the sofa, anger bubbled up inside of Jem. He might not like Mel, but even she didn't deserve this knob.

His claws extended, and the magic he'd been holding in check welled up, demanding to be set free. All thoughts of acting like a "normal cat" fled his mind as he considered the most creative way to put the man in his place.

A mocking sneer from Derek was the last straw needed to push him over the edge. Jem gathered his magic to him and prepared to –

"Jem!" Mel stood in the doorway, her blue eyes blazing.

Oh so slowly, he let the magic fizzle away. It was clear from her furious expression that she'd sensed the buildup of energy. What were the chances he could pass it off as a figment of her imagination?

The douchebag boyfriend chose that moment to pipe up. "I don't know what happened. I was just going to pet him and he freaked out."

Jem looked at him in utter disbelief. The mask had snapped back into place the second Mel entered the room, and Derek was now the picture of innocence. Surely she wasn't naïve enough to fall for this crap?

But it turned out she was.

Mel hurried into the room, apologising profusely as she ran her hands over Derek and checked him for any sign of injury while the man simpered.

Jem watched it all, stunned. Okay, he'd been wrong to risk exposing them with magic. He knew that. But how could she not see the act this guy was putting on?

"I think you should go to your room," Mel said in a cool voice, finally turning her attention to him.

He searched her face for any sign that she recognised the boyfriend's lie for what it was, any hint of doubt in his guilt. There was nothing. She believed the knobhead boyfriend, and that was it.

Hurt flashed through him, but he pushed it away, reaching instead for the anger that had been bubbling beneath the surface. With a hiss, he stalked from the room. He needed to find that damn catnip.

# CHAPTER FIVE

J em cringed away from the sunlight, burying his face in Mr. Fluffles to save him from the evil bright light that was trying to drag him back to reality. How was it morning already? His head pounded, and for the briefest moment, he half-regretted his catnip binge the night before. Only half, though.

In the end, the catnip had been pathetically easy to find. The witch had left it out on the kitchen counter, apparently planning to make good on her promise despite the sauce incident. After indulging until the early hours of the morning, he'd finally managed to put his anger aside for long enough to fall into a drunken stupor. Now, that anger was replaced by a twinge of unease.

Given how bright it was, it was clear Mel hadn't bothered to wake him for breakfast, or their planned morning lesson. Likely she was still in a mood over last night and didn't want to talk to him. And while that would normally suit him down to the ground, he was uncomfortably aware that she could report him to FFS for his near transgression in front of the human.

Screw that. She'd damn well listen to his side of the story first!

With that thought spurring him on, Jem rolled out of bed with all the grace of a drunk possum. The room swayed, and it took a couple of moments to set everything to rights. When he was seeing straight again, he pushed the bedroom door open and padded into the hall.

The ladder extended up into the attic, confirming his suspicion that Mel had gone ahead with her day without him. Was she up there right now, considering whether or not to contact FFS?

He debated "accidentally" bumping into the ladder and knocking it over. If she was stranded up there, she couldn't call anyone and she'd have no choice but to hear him out. That was, of course, assuming she hadn't brought her phone up with her, and really the ceiling wasn't high enough to make it more than a little inconvenient for her to get down. Yeah, he should probably come up with a better plan.

Steeling himself for the lecture that was no doubt to come, Jem cleared the distance to the ceiling in a single leap and landed in the middle of the pentagram. Bullseye.

"Flipping heck." Mel jerked back at his sudden

31

appearance, and her hand struck a glass jar that was open on the oak table in front of her.

He watched in amusement as she scrambled to catch it before it could fall or spill its contents.

"Dammit, Jem. I'm going to get you a kitty bell if you keep sneaking up on people like that." With visibly shaking hands, she carefully righted the jar and stepped away from the table.

Jem took in the array of jars that lined the table, and the purple notebook open next to them. A small black cauldron bubbled away in the centre of it all, and the faint citrus aroma tickled his nose. Curious, he padded over and jumped up on the table for a closer look.

Mel looked like she might actually have an apoplexy and hurried to sweep anything breakable out of his reach. He guessed she was still sore over the jar of sauce after all.

"What's this?" He nudged the purple notebook with a paw. "Let me guess. You're working on a beauty potion because you found a grey hair? Or is it a love potion so you can find a better boyfriend than Douchebag Derek?"

One that didn't abuse animals would be a good start, but he didn't say that since she wouldn't believe him anyway.

Without answering, Mel snatched the notebook away before he could catch a glimpse of anything interesting. He turned his attention back to the jars instead.

The one closest to him was empty except for a

dusting of orange powder at the bottom. A small white label showed the words "phoenix feather" in neat print. He did a double take and read it again to make sure he hadn't been mistaken.

"That's a restricted ingredient." He gave a sly smirk. "Who's been a naughty witch?"

Mel scowled at him. "Can you please get down off the table before you break something important?"

"Like what?" He padded over to the next jar, whose label declared the scattering of leaves at the bottom to be belladonna. "This?"

"Don't do that," she snapped, grabbing the jar and moving it out of his reach again.

That was yet another ingredient from the restricted list – a list of ingredients that were either extremely rare, potentially lethal if prepared wrong, or in some cases, both.

Access to restricted ingredients was closely monitored by both FFS and the High Council of Covens, the other ruling faction within the magic world. Only witches that held particular roles and had proven themselves to be at a sufficient level of competence had access to them. Mel might be talented for her age, but he highly doubted she fell into that category.

"Interesting setup you have here," he mused. "You like to come across all holier-than-thou, but in reality you're up here doing Hecate knows what with your no doubt illegally acquired ingredients. Maybe FFS should be more worried about you than me."

Mel opened and closed her mouth like a bewildered fish, then shut it and planted her hands on her hips. She blew out a frustrated breath that caused strands of her purple hair to float in the air for a moment.

"If you must know, I'm working on my submission for my coven entrance trial. All of these ingredients have been logged and registered."

"Coven entrance?" He blinked in surprise. "You're one of *those* witches."

There were two ways a witch could stabilise and strengthen their magic once they reached maturity – by bonding with a familiar or by joining a coven and garnering strength from a combined group of witches. The coven route was a fairly modern convention that had come about when some witches had grown jealous of the fact their familiar's power surpassed their own so greatly. It was an institution built on a foundation of greed, cleverly marketed as a forward-thinking alternative to the tradition of the witch-familiar bond.

"What do you mean '*those* witches?'" Mel demanded, her shoulders stiffening at his words. "Do you have a problem with the covens?"

He sneered. "You mean, do I have a problem with a load of jumped-up witches with a superiority complex? No, not at all."

She flinched. "What would you know about the covens?" she said quietly, turning away to organise the already orderly rows of jars she'd moved aside.

"I know more than enough." Like, FFS was entrusting a witch who didn't even believe in the witch-familiar bond with his last chance before they stripped him of everything that made him who he was.

He flicked his tail in irritation and turned to jump off the table. His tail connected with something solid, and Mel's panicked gasp was followed by an ominous crash.

Jem cringed and turned slowly, expecting to see a broken jar. He froze.

The small black cauldron that had been bubbling away now lay on its side, a thick, orangey substance oozing out across the table. Mel stood staring at it in wide-eyed horror, her knuckles white as she gripped the edge of the table.

Squirming, he was about to ask if she'd needed that for tonight's dinner when he saw it – the orangey substance coating her fingers.

"Eh, what potion did you say you were working on?"

Mel blinked dumbly at him, then looked down at her hands. All the colour leeched from her face and she released the table, stumbling backwards.

"Oh god." She wiped her hands frantically against her top, smearing orange streaks over her chest.

Jem watched with a sense of morbid fascination as she danced around the room, growing more and more agitated. Humans could be so overdramatic.

He was about to tell her to calm down and go wash her hands instead of jumping around like a lunatic when he felt it. The tingle of magic. It skittered across his fur like static electricity, and expanded to fill the room with that citrus aroma.

Mel froze, her panicked movements abruptly ceasing as her eyes grew wide. Then she started to shrink.

# CHAPTER SIX

W*ell, this is new*, Jem thought to himself as he watched Mel turn from human-sized to Barbie-sized in a matter of seconds. A very angry, scary-looking Barbie.

He gave an awkward cough and plonked his arse down on the table. "So, that's what you were working on? Not bad, I suppose."

"Oh my god. Look what you've done!" Mel gestured wildly up at him from the floor, where she now stood barely a foot tall. "What the hell am I going to do?"

He eyed the miniature human in fascination as she continued her rant. It was almost too tempting not to swat her with his paw to see how easy she was to knock over, but given how irate she currently was, and the fact that FFS might not be too pleased with this new development, it was probably ill-advised.

Instead, he surreptitiously licked his paw to make

sure none of the potion had landed on him. "What's the problem? Just reverse the spell."

"I CAN'T just reverse the spell," she shrieked up at him, her face turning puce. "I don't have the ingredients."

He froze mid-lick, an uneasy feeling trickling over his fur. "What do you mean you don't have the ingredients?"

"This is a level seven spell," she said, her voice somehow growing even more high-pitched with each word. "All the core ingredients are on the restricted list."

He shrugged, ignoring the unease that was growing ever stronger. "So, get them from the coven stores. They approved your request for these ingredients. They'll have to approve a request for the reversal ones."

Typical witch, making a big deal about nothing. There was no need to get so hysterical over a little mishap. Besides, she should really be more careful about leaving her potions lying around; he'd provided a valuable teaching point, if you asked him.

Mel wrung her hands and paced with growing agitation. "You don't understand. All ingredients I access are logged. If they see that I've requested the reversal ingredients, they'll know I messed up. They'll never accept me into the coven then."

He snorted and muttered under his breath, "Looks like I've done you a favour, so."

Apparently he hadn't spoken as quietly as he

thought because she halted her army march, and oh so slowly, turned her teeny tiny doll-like head to face him.

"This. Is. All. Your. Fault."

He could see the moment the true realisation of her situation dawned on her, and her expression settled into one of hard resolve. He backed away slowly.

His hind legs met with air as they moved off the edge of the table, and he scrambled to regain his balance, digging his claws into the wood to stop himself from falling. After a moment, he righted himself, only to notice the deep scratches he'd made with his claws. Oops. He plonked his furry arse down on top of them – nothing to see here, nope, nothing at all.

"Now, look. There's really no need to go pointing fingers and assigning blame. This has all been a terrible misunderstanding. I'm sure we can –"

A sudden buzzing on the table sent him leaping into the air. This time he failed to save himself and found his feet just in time to land on the ground next to a very pissed pint-sized Mel.

"That's my phone, Jem. Someone is sending me a message, and I'll never be able to read it because I'm ten freakin' inches high and I can't reach the top of my table anymore."

He cringed away from the hysterical witch.

Okay, so the situation wasn't ideal. He could admit that. But it was probably just her knobhead boyfriend messaging, anyway; there was really no need to get so upset over the phone. He'd read the stupid message for her and then they could get back to finding a solution like calm, rational beings – preferably one that didn't involve him being magically castrated.

Jem leaped back up onto the table and swatted at the small buzzing contraption with his paw. It took a couple of attempts before the screen flashed on to reveal a picture of Mel with another smiling brown-haired woman. A message preview showed above it.

The message was cut off after the first couple of lines, but he didn't need to see any more to realise how fucked he was. Dread settled like a brick in his stomach.

"Well," Mel snapped. "What does it say?"

Jem's tongue darted out nervously as he stared at the screen. If he looked for long enough, maybe it would change? Maybe he'd started hallucinating from an over-indulgence of catnip?

"It, eh, it's a reminder for the first FFS inspection tomorrow."

The silence that met his comment was so charged it almost made his fur stand on end.

He'd forgotten all about the bloody inspections.

Somehow he didn't think FFS would be too amused by the newly diminutive size of his trainer. He needed to fix this A.S.A.P. And he needed to make sure the witch didn't rat him out once he had.

"So, look, this has been fun and all, but how about we get you back to your proper size so we can get started on some of that really useful training you have planned?"

Even without looking, he could feel Mel glare up at him. He squirmed.

He really didn't see what the big deal was. If the covens were stupid enough to refuse admission to a witch of her calibre simply for requesting the reversal ingredients, then it proved that they didn't deserve her.

Unfortunately, Mel wasn't quite ready to see his way of thinking just yet.

"I will not ruin my chances with the coven over this," she said, her voice going scarily calm. "You caused this. Now, you damned well better fix it, Jem."

He blinked. What was *he* meant to do? She knew enough about familiars to know his magic couldn't negate a potion she'd created. Did she expect him to pull an antidote out of his arse?

"I don't exactly have my stash of illegally acquired potion ingredients on me at this point in time," he told her, unable to help the hint of sarcasm that crept into his tone.

She raised an eyebrow. "That's too bad. I'll just have to explain the situation to the FFS inspector tomorrow so that they can get me the ingredients I require."

"Wow. Hold up. Let's not be so hasty." He scrambled for a solution that might placate her, but there was only one he could think of. It was the last thing he wanted to consider, but he couldn't afford to fail the very first inspection. "I don't have the ingredients you need. But I do know where you can get them."

"Where?" she demanded, sounding oh so cute with

her teeny tiny bossy voice – he really did want to swat her.

He straightened, emboldened by the eagerness that fuelled her question. Mel might not want to look bad in front of the covens, but he had a feeling she wouldn't want to ruin her reputation with FFS either. She'd worked hard to get to where she was, and though she'd ask FFS for help if she had no other choice, she'd be reluctant to admit that a lowly familiar like him had gotten the best of her.

"Promise to help me pass the inspection tomorrow, and I'll tell you."

She opened her mouth to speak, and he jumped in quickly to sweeten the deal before she could refuse.

"I'll even help you get them."

She was quiet for long enough that his confidence started to wane and he was beginning to wonder if he might have to debase himself by begging.

Finally, she nodded. "Fine. Tell me where, and as soon as the inspection is done, you are helping me to get them or so help me Hecate..."

He sagged with relief. So long as she helped him pass the inspection, he'd live to fight another day. Of course, he might not last much longer than that considering where they'd be going. But that was a problem for future Jem.

"Where else does one acquire restricted ingredients illegally?" he said. "The black market."

## CHAPTER SEVEN

As it turned out, Mel wasn't too keen on his suggestion that they visit the black market. She agreed to table the discussion while they dealt with the more immediate problem of the inspection, though, and he was sure he could bring her around to his way of thinking – eventually.

"Can we not just tell the inspector you're trying out a new look?" he groused, floating a jar of dried sage down to the floor where Mel was ticking items off her neatly composed list. "When you do things like that with your hair, will they really be surprised?"

Okay, so shrinking yourself wasn't quite the same as colouring your hair bright purple, but who knew what the kids of today were up to?

Mel glared up at him, clearly affronted. "My hair change runes are in high demand, I'll have you know.

And no, we cannot just tell them 'I'm trying a new look.' Now, get me the hibiscus and blackberries."

Hair change runes? He'd heard it all now! With an unimpressed harrumph, he found the next two jars and swatted them off the shelf with his tail.

Mel gave a panicked shriek as the requested ingredients tumbled towards her.

He allowed himself the split second of amusement before catching them on a bed of air with his magic and lowering them the last inch or so to the floor. How many more bloody ingredients did she need anyway? He was getting tired and needed a snack.

"So, how exactly are these things going to help me pass the inspection? Are you planning to knock the inspector out before they can realise how small you are?" Now, there was an idea… It could work.

Mel grimaced, and Jem could've sworn she muttered, "I really hope not," under her breath, but all she said out loud was, "You'll see."

An hour later, fed up and still none the wiser, he flopped over onto his back and groaned. "I quit. Let them take my magic. Just FEED ME."

Mel nudged him in the side with a tiny, pointy elbow. "Oh, stop whining. We're done. I have everything we need."

He leapt to his feet, half afraid she'd change her mind. Quicker than you could say "catnip," he ran to the opening in the floor and bounded down the ladder.

"Eh, Jem?" Mel called, the slight tremor in her voice causing him to skid to a stop. "Need a little help here."

Hungry and irritated, he looked back to find Mel peering down from the ceiling opening. Her legs dangled over the side, not far from the top rung of the ladder, but she clung to the edge for all she was worth and her face was ashen.

He sighed. "You're not going to tell me you're afraid of heights, are you?"

"There's a big difference when you suddenly find yourself shrunk to less than a fifth of your original height," she snapped.

A twinge of guilt stopped him from making any further comment. With a twitch of his nose, he floated a flailing Mel to the floor, then turned impatiently to the stairs. If he didn't get something to eat soon, he'd have to resort to snacking on her. And then he'd really have something to feel guilty about.

He started down the steps, waiting for the inevitable request for more help. When none came, he turned to look back, curious.

Mel's face was red and the muscles in her arms were straining as she lowered herself down a step. Given her size, each one looked like a miniature mountain next to her, but she'd made it down the first few without a word of complaint. Grudgingly impressed by her determination, he waited for her to catch up with him so that he could at least catch her if she took a tumble.

They had finally made it – slowly – to the bottom when there was a rhythmic knock on the door. A moment later, Jem heard the jangle of a key in the lock.

Mel? It's me." A woman in her mid-twenties with long brown hair pushed open the door and peeked her head inside.

Jem recognised her as the woman from Mel's screensaver and noted that her aura bore the unusual rainbow colour of a witch's. Idly, he wondered who she was and whether or not she had any food with her.

The woman halted when she saw Jem in the hallway, and then her eyes fell on the pint-sized Mel at his side. Her mouth fell open.

"Holy Hecate, you weren't joking when you said you had a problem, were you?"

Mel's cheeks turned rosy pink as she muttered, "Hey, Elena. Thanks for coming so quickly."

Elena slipped inside and closed the door behind her. "Right." She clapped her hands together. "Into the kitchen, both of you. I'll make the tea while you fill me in."

Jem bristled, instinctively wanting to rebel against being ordered around. Then his stomach gave an angry grumble and he decided that stubbornness could wait. He followed the two witches.

Without waiting to be asked, Elena scooped Mel up and got her settled safely on the kitchen island. She then set about making some chamomile tea only to realise Mel wouldn't be able to drink from the mug, and spent a further five minutes searching for a straw. By the time she placed an open tin of tuna in front of Jem, he was about ready to chew her hand off.

He only half listened as Mel brought the other

witch up to date on their predicament, his attention focused on making sure every last bit of fish made it into his mouth.

"Can you not just reschedule the FFS inspection until after you've gotten the ingredients?" Elena asked when Mel finished.

"They'd know something was wrong. Plus, if we're actually going to do this" – Mel glared unhappily in Jem's direction – "we'll need time to figure out where the black market will be next. It moves around every full moon, and the next one is tomorrow."

Elena let out a low whistle. "I didn't even think the black market was real. My mother used to tell me stories about witches who went there and were never seen again. I always assumed it was an urban legend or something."

Jem cringed and carefully avoided looking at Mel. This witch was not helping. Yes, the black market was dangerous, but how else were they going to get the ingredients for the reversal? The last thing he needed was for Elena to freak Mel out so much that she changed her mind about their deal.

Luckily, Elena didn't elaborate any further on the horror stories she'd been told, and instead switched to the practicalities of their plan. "Okay. What do you need me to do?"

"We need you to be me for the inspection," Mel said, quickly holding up her hands as her friend's eyes widened. "I'll guide you on everything you need to know to get through it, and I have an illusion tonic brewing, so we'll only have to make some temporary changes to your appearance."

Elena chewed on her lip, considering this. Suddenly, she looked worried. "Will I have to do magic?"

Jem looked at her in surprise, noting the sympathy that shone in Mel's eyes as she reached over and patted the other witch's hand. What was that all about?

"I'll do the magic work," Mel reassured her. "All you have to do is answer a few questions to keep the inspector happy. It's only been a few days, so they won't be expecting much progress with the training."

Still seeming slightly unsure, Elena agreed.

With that settled, Mel set about explaining the structure the inspection would take. Jem tried his best to look like he was paying attention, but it was so damn boring. Before long, his head was drooping and thoughts of a nap called to him like a siren song. He drifted into a glorious daydream involving sushi, catnip, and that hot ginger tabby he'd spotted across the street.

Something bopped him hard on the nose and he jerked his head up, belatedly realising – thanks to her irritated glare – that Mel had been talking to him.

"Eh, I agree?"

Her scowl deepened, and he had to resist the urge to snicker. She looked almost cute, like a grumpy little doll. Of course, that grumpy little doll could sign his metaphorical death warrant if she got too pissed off, so he attempted to look suitably apologetic.

"I need my calligraphy pen. Can you please make yourself useful and get it for me while I get Elena ready?" she repeated.

He huffed out a sigh. Did he have to do everything? Sure, she was a bit more vertically challenged than usual, but she had magic too. Grumbling to himself, he closed his eyes and sent his magic outwards to search for the object they needed.

"Jem," she snapped. "I didn't say go back to –"

She cut off abruptly as a wooden calligraphy pen appeared on the countertop in front of her. It was a beautiful, rich mahogany colour and had intricate runes carved into its surface. The nib was silver and had similar swirling patterns etched into it.

"Oh."

Jem smirked. "This what you're looking for?"

She opened her mouth and snapped it closed again. "Thank you."

It took a bit of manoeuvring, but after a couple of tries, Mel managed to pick up the pen and angle it in a way that would allow her to write. She turned to Elena.

"Where would you like the rune?"

Elena considered for a moment, then rolled up her sleeve to reveal swirling black tattoos. She held out her arm, palm up, to display a bare patch of skin.

Fascinated, Jem watched as Mel used the pen to draw a complex series of lines in the spot indicated, a strangely iridescent ink flowing from the silver nib. With each line she completed, Elena's hair changed colour a shade at a time.

By the time the final line was drawn, Elena's hair was a vibrant purple that perfectly matched Mel's. It brought her heart-shaped face to life and even though the transformation wasn't yet complete, even Jem had to admit it suited her.

"I've always wanted to try purple hair." She ran her fingers through the newly coloured strands, her blue eyes sparkling with excitement as she admired them.

Mel dropped the pen to the countertop with a heavy exhale. She wiped the back of her hand across her forehead. "You could always keep it like that after this whole fiasco is over."

Elena beamed. "What's next?"

# CHAPTER EIGHT

Tick. Tick. Tick. The clock on the kitchen wall continued its ominous countdown. Just a few more minutes until the inspector was due to arrive, and they'd find out one way or the other whether this crazy plan was going to work.

Mel was busy making the finishing touches to her illusion potion while Elena watched, chewing her fingernails to the quick. Jem would've been worried about the witch's obvious nerves, but he was working hard to think about anything other than his upcoming doom.

"How long will it last?" Elena asked, shifting on her stool so much he was about to ask her if she had fleas.

"About an hour," Mel answered, not looking up from the small glass container she was stirring. "After that, it will begin to wear off gradually. The changes from the runes will last until the runes are cancelled, so that should slow the visual change a bit."

Jem had to admit her idea to make some of the key physical changes with runes had been a good one. Illusion potions were notoriously volatile, so to have the simpler cosmetic changes – such as hair and eye colour – done by runes allowed for a modicum of stability. The work she'd done had been impressively intricate, and few witches could've managed it. He'd never have acknowledged that out loud, of course.

Mel stepped back from her preparations and looked up at her friend. "Okay, you remember what I told you?"

Elena nodded. "Keep physical contact with the inspector to a minimum. Speak like I know what I'm talking about. Get him out as quickly as possible."

Mel turned to him then, hands on her hips and eyebrows raised expectantly. "And you?"

"Will be on my best behaviour."

Looking less than reassured by his statement, Mel glanced at the clock. "The inspector will be here in ten minutes." She nudged the glass of luminous green liquid towards Elena. "Bottoms up."

Elena scrunched her nose in disgust but downed the concoction in one go.

At first, nothing happened. Then the air around her grew hazy.

Instinctively, Jem blinked to try and clear his vision even though he knew it was the potion causing the visual distortion. When his eyes opened after the second blink, he did a double take.

Mel was sitting before him. Only, it wasn't Mel. It was Elena overladen with the illusion of Mel's form.

The two witches were already of a similar size – or at least they had been before the unfortunate accident that he might or might not have been responsible for. The rune work had changed Elena's brown hair to vibrant purple and adjusted the shade of her blue eyes to match Mel's. And the tattoos that snaked around Elena's left arm were easily covered with a long-sleeved top.

Now, however, the witch's very structure appeared altered too. Her heart-shaped face had evened to a softer oval, her nose had lost its button-like appearance, and her curvaceous figure had hardened to a more athletic physique. Even knowing it was an illusion, Jem struggled to tell the difference.

He was thinking that they might actually have a chance of pulling this off when the doorbell chimed.

Elena's eyes widened in fear, and his stomach plummeted. If this witch didn't get her shit together, he was screwed.

"Right. Places, everyone." Mel clapped her hands together.

This snapped Elena to attention. Giving herself a brisk shake, she picked Mel up from the island countertop and placed her in the cupboard where they'd agreed she would hide for the duration of the inspection.

While she wouldn't be able to interfere directly, the witch-familiar bond had given him and Mel a telepathic link that he pointedly ignored under any other circumstances. Today, however, it would come in handy if things started going sideways; with her in hearing range, she should hopefully be able to give them a nudge to get back on track.

Once Mel was safely ensconced between the obscenely colourful plates, Elena hurried to answer the door. Jem padded along behind her, more than ready to get this circus show over with.

Elena swung the door open with more force than necessary, revealing a good-looking blond man dressed in a crisp white shirt and grey slacks. He was carrying a black clipboard in one hand, and he offered the other in greeting with a friendly smile.

"Melanie Blackwood? I'm Ciaran, head of the FFS monitoring division."

She stared at the hand as if it might bite her, and after a long, awkward minute, Ciaran took pity on her and dropped the offending appendage.

He gestured past her, into the hallway. "May I?"

Almost tripping over her feet, Elena stepped back to open the door wider. "Sorry. Of course. Please, come in."

Jem barely refrained from putting his head in his paws. He might as well hand himself over to FFS on a silver platter. What had Mel been thinking when she got this witch involved?

Thankfully, it appeared the inspector didn't already

know Mel, which meant he didn't have any precon-ceived notions of what she was like. It was concerning – and maybe a little flattering – that FFS had seen fit to send the head of the monitoring division, but hopefully he'd overlook some of Elena's eccentricities as simply being Mel's quirky personality.

Speaking of eccentricities – the witch babbled non-stop as she led the inspector through to the kitchen. "Make yourself at home," she said, waving to the stools around the island. "Can I get you tea? Coffee? Some-thing stronger?"

Jem glared at her. What happened to sticking to the plan? Get the inspector in, get him out. Don't encourage him to bloody move in!

Ciaran gave her a reserved smile as he settled on a stool. "I'm okay, thanks. I won't take up more of your time than necessary."

The inspector placed his clipboard on the counter. He flipped over a page and pulled a pen out of his jacket pocket. Scribbling something at the top, he turned his attention to Jem.

"Jeremiah Snufflekins, I presume?"

*Do you see any other cats around here?*

Jem gave an unimpressed "Reow," as he eyed the clipboard. Had they been transported back to the Stone Age at some point while he wasn't looking? Surely FFS could afford to shell out for laptops for their employees.

"How has everything being going?" Ciaran asked, directing the question to both him and Elena.

"Oh, great. It's all been great," Elena jumped in.

Was Jem imagining it, or had her voice gone a few octaves higher than normal? He flicked her leg with his tail and scowled. *Dammit, woman. Pull yourself together!*

Elena blinked at him, then seemed to catch herself. Abruptly, she sat up taller and placed her hands on her lap to stop their fidgeting. "I mean, obviously it's a work in progress, but Jem has been very cooperative."

Ciaran scribbled something on the page, nodding to show he was listening. "And the familiar bond was successfully established?"

"Oh, yes siree. All established. No issues whatsoever."

This time, the overenthusiastic response earned her a raised eyebrow from the inspector. Jem idly wondered if they could just kill the man and dispose of the body; that would be less painful for all involved – the inspector included.

"Any behavioural concerns?" Ciaran glanced sideways at Jem, as if aware of the direction his thoughts had taken. "Mr. Snufflekins appears to have quite a colourful record by all accounts."

Jem hissed. They could definitely get away with disposing of the body.

"Concerns? Nope. None. Jem has been a star pupil. Best I ever had."

Even Jem couldn't blame the inspector for the sceptical look that settled on his face at this. No one was stupid enough to believe that a familiar with his record was going to suddenly change his ways – not even with the threat of a magical lobotomy hanging over them.

Worried that they were threading into dangerous territory, Jem decided a little reminder of the plan was in order. He allowed his claws to extend and gave Elena a sharp poke in the shin.

She gave a startled yelp, quickly covering her mouth with both hands.

At Ciaran's surprised look, she cowered meekly into herself. "Sorry, thought I saw a mouse."

Her cheeks glowed crimson, and when the inspector finally returned his gaze back to his clip-board, she glared down at Jem. He glared back.

Elena was the one to break eye contact first. Once more, she straightened up and pasted a smile on her face. "As I'm sure you can appreciate, inspector –"

"Please. Call me Ciaran."

"Ciaran," she repeated, losing her stride for a moment. "As I'm sure you can appreciate, Jem and I are still in the early stages of getting to know each other. I don't have any concerns regarding his behaviour, so I've really got nothing to report at this point. If you'd like to contact me again in another week, perhaps I can give you a more detailed report?"

"Of course." Ciaran nodded agreeably. "If we could run a couple of quick drills, then I'll be out of your hair."

"Drills?" Even through the illusion, Elena's face paled noticeably. "I don't suppose you mean math drills?"

Ciaran laughed. "No, I wouldn't torture you like that. I just need to conduct some basic workings between the two of you to confirm the bond is in place. Standard procedure. I'm sure you're well used to it."

"Oh, sure." Her eyes darted around as if seeking an exit to flee by, and her hands clenched together so tightly in her lap that her knuckles blanched.

Jem raced through the options available. Mel had told them that strict procedure required the inspector to validate the bond. Her long-standing and stellar reputation with the FFS meant – current inspector excepted – all simply took her word as verification rather than wasting time with tests. They'd expected the same to be the case today.

Given the early stage of the rehabilitation, it was unlikely that any of the tests would be too difficult for him to blag. But Jem suddenly remembered the panicked deer in headlights look on Elena's face when she'd asked if magic would be involved. Why hadn't he pushed to find out what her problem was?

He was just considering staging a distraction when the illusion around Elena flickered. He blinked.

It happened again.

One minute he was staring at Mel's double, the next he could see a panic-stricken Elena with a foggy haze around her. Once. Twice. Three times.

What the hell? Illusion spells didn't fade this way. And, anyway, they should have had at least another half an hour yet.

Jem darted a glance towards the inspector, but the

man was too busy with his clipboard to have noticed the glitching witch. It was only a matter of time before he did, however.

*Mel*, Jem called urgently through the bond. *There's something wrong with your potion.*

A soft thud sounded from the cupboard where Mel was hiding, and a litany of PG profanities came to him through the bond. Jem wanted to laugh at the image of her bumping her head in the cramped space, but he was too busy resigning himself to his fate as a magic-less familiar.

The noise hadn't gone unnoticed by Ciaran, who glanced at the cupboard, eyebrows raised. "Um, is there something in there?"

"Oh, no, nothing. Just a mousetrap going off. Turns out not all cats are good hunters," Elena babbled, laughing nervously. "About these tests you wanted to run..."

"What?" he asked, frowning at the cupboard before turning his attention back to her. "Oh, yes. Nothing too difficult. We'll confirm and measure the strength of the bond between you and Mr. Snufflekins. That way we can map out our future inspections more efficiently."

The illusion glitched again.

Ciaran blinked a couple of times and rubbed his eyes, clearly thinking they were playing tricks on him. He shook his head. "Why don't we get started?"

Elena looked at Jem, the desperate plea clear on her face: *Do something.*

What did she expect him to do?

He considered making a run for it, but before he could make a decision – rash or otherwise – the illusion flickered and winked out entirely.

"What the –" Ciaran pushed back from the table, his brow furrowed in confusion.

Jem dashed between his feet and sent him stumbling.

Clearly not on board with Jem's spur-of-the-moment plan to induce a concussion, Elena reached out to grab the man. Her hand made contact with his arm, and there was a flash of blinding light.

Jem hissed and turned away.

Light seared his vision, and for the longest moment, he was completely blind, unable to see anything besides a glaring white. Slowly, the kitchen came back into focus and the light faded. He turned around to see exactly what had happened.

And found the inspector slumped in a heap on the ground.

## CHAPTER NINE

"Is he dead?" Jem prodded the unconscious inspector with his paw, ignoring the glower Mel gave him from the far side of the body.

Elena paced up and down the kitchen, wringing her hands together. "I didn't mean to do it. Oh god, this is such a mess."

Mel stepped into her path and held up her hands. "Let's not panic. Why don't you calm down and explain to us exactly what happened?"

Miraculously, Elena halted her stride before she paced right over her friend. She bit her lip, suddenly looking sheepish. "It's just a little sleep spell. That's all."

"A sleep spell?"

Elena nodded. "It happens sometimes when I get nervous. I wish people would leave me alone, and *poof,* they're asleep."

Jem stared at the witch. Was she serious? How was

that even possible? He'd been right here the whole time, and he knew for a fact she hadn't used a potion or even an incantation. It was almost as if she'd used her magic instinctively, the same way a familiar did. He'd never heard of a witch doing that before, especially not one with no familiar bond of their own to draw on.

Worryingly, Mel didn't seem the slightest bit surprised by the revelation her friend had magically roofied the head of the FFS monitoring division. She simply asked, "How long does it normally last?"

"No more than twelve hours, usually." Elena blushed, clearly realising how bad it sounded that she had enough experience with similar situations to gauge it by.

Mel considered this, then nodded. "It doesn't give us much time, but it'll have to do. Jem, can you move the inspector into the living room and make him more comfortable? Elena, grab my magical handcuffs from the top floor."

Jem was about to tell her to move the dead body herself when the second part of what she said registered with him. Magical handcuffs? Now, wasn't this interesting. Someone's halo was looking a little less shiny all of a sudden.

Pointedly ignoring his smirk, Mel followed Elena out of the kitchen, leaving Jem alone with the "sleeping" inspector.

He stared at the meat sack on the floor beside him and gave an irritated huff. Did she appreciate how hard it was to lift a dead weight of this size? Sure, his magic was powerful, but he damned well better be getting a snack after this.

With more strain than he cared to admit, he raised the body an inch off the floor and moved it towards the door. Jem could only hope the sleeping spell the man was under protected him from concussion because at least one of those knocks to the head sounded painful. By the time he reached the living room and dumped the inspector unceremoniously on the sofa, his paws were damp with sweat and he was about tapped out.

Jem had just slumped to the floor when Mel and Elena returned. Elena was carrying a delicate silver chain in her hand, and with Mel's help, secured it around the inspector so that his ankles and wrists were bound together.

"Is this really necessary?" Elena chewed her lip, guilt written all over her face.

Mel gave her a reassuring smile. "It's only a precaution. The full moon was last night, so the black market should be set up in its new location by now. Me and Jem will find its location, get the ingredients we need, and be back before the inspector wakes up. I can tell him he took a funny turn during the inspection and collapsed. We've never met before today, so he won't know if my behaviour was off, and hopefully he'll put anything strange down to the unfortunate bump on his head."

Jem ducked his head down, trying not to look guilty. At least she seemed more agreeable to visiting the black market now.

"What if he wakes before you get back?" Elena asked.

Mel's smile faltered. "We'll figure that out if it happens. For now, I need you to stay here and watch over him. Just in case. Can you do that for me?"

Still looking uncertain, Elena nodded.

With that agreed, Mel gestured for Jem to follow her back to the kitchen. He wasn't too sure that leaving Elena alone with a defenceless man was a good idea, but considering option B – kill the inspector and dispose of his body – was still a distinct possibility, he figured it made no difference.

He padded into the kitchen after Mel, and without waiting for her to ask, floated her up to the island where her laptop was waiting. Though his magic was still sluggish after moving the inspector, he threw in a loop-the-loop or two to amuse himself.

"Eek. Jem! Stop it. Dammit, put me down."

At her request, he plonked her down next to her laptop. She glared at him, red-faced and somewhat dishevelled. He blinked innocently up at her and leapt up to settle on the counter. She couldn't expect him to give up having fun altogether, could she?

With a low growl, she shook her head and turned her attention to the laptop.

"Explain to me again how this works."

He raised an eyebrow, unable to help himself. "You're the one with the magical handcuffs. Are you really telling me you've never played in the dark pits of the magic world?"

Stony silence was her only response.

"Fine. Fine." He huffed. "First, we need to get onto Magiweb. Then you're going to use those fantastic brain cells of yours to get us through the digital labyrinth. Assuming we do all that right, and you don't get your hard drive fried, it should give us the address for the dark market."

"My hard drive is going to get fried?"

He waved her concern away with a paw. "Only if you screw up."

Her eyes all but bugged out of her head, and he sighed. "I'll tell you what to do. Just don't press any random buttons with those freakily small hands of yours. Now, if you'd be so good as to open a web browser so we can get this done before the dead guy wakes up."

She shook her head, but did as he asked. Once the browser had loaded up, she looked at him expectantly. "What now?"

"Type 'Hocus Pocus sucks' into the search bar."

She gaped at him. "You're not serious?"

"Oh, I'm deadly serious. It does suck."

The look of indignation on her face almost made him laugh. Witches were so predictable.

With a scowl, she typed the words and hit Enter. The screen turned black.

Her hands froze in place and her face paled. "Did I break –"

Before she could finish the sentence, the screen flicked back on. The search engine looked almost exactly as it had a moment ago, only now there was a weird shimmery quality overlaying it. The shimmer was a privacy spell that ensured their location and identity couldn't be traced while they were connected.

Along the left-hand side of the screen, adverts scrolled by offering services that might appeal to magic users with a questionable sense of scruples: guaranteed untraceable death potions, custom-made voodoo dolls, tax evasion charms.

"Welcome to Magiweb," he said. "I hope you're ready to get your hands dirty."

# CHAPTER TEN

I t took more than an hour for them the crack the codes and riddles that concealed the black market's location. The last one in particular had been a doozie. Finally, an address flashed up on the screen. Two seconds and it was gone, but it had been enough. Jem knew where they needed to go, and he didn't like it one bit.

He groaned and flopped down onto the counter. Did he really need his magic? Normal cats seemed happy enough to laze about the house all day; maybe he could just do that?

Mel frowned at the now black screen, then turned her wary gaze on him. "Is that bad?"

"Is it bad? Damn right it's bad."

She waited for him to elaborate, and he buried his head in his paws.

"We have to get the bus," he wailed.

There was a moment of shocked silence, then she barked out a laugh. "That's it? You made it sound like we'd have to traverse the pits of hell. I'd at least expected you to say the place was dangerous."

He raised his head to gape at her. Had the shrinking potion affected her brain capacity too?

"Well, of course it's going to be dangerous. It's the black market. Do you know how bad public transport smells when your senses are as fine-tuned as mine? And let me tell you, you'll be getting up close and personal with some interesting things now that you're all miniature."

She rolled her eyes. "We'll just have to suck it up. Won't we? Let's finalise the plan so we can get moving. It'll be dark by six, and I'd really prefer to be back before then."

So would he. The black market wasn't a safe place for familiars; he didn't want to spend any more time there than he had to.

His stomach grumbled uneasily, reminding him he hadn't eaten in the last hour.

"I need a snack before we go," he told Mel, pushing down his nerves.

Her eyes widened in disbelief as he used his magic to open the cupboard and float a tin of tuna over to rest next to him on the counter. He needed to be at full strength for what was to come.

Once he'd fuelled up and they'd planned the best route, Mel went to check that Elena had everything under control with their hostage. The man was still breathing, at least, but Jem hadn't yet decided if that was a good thing.

Ominous black clouds filled the sky as they stepped outside, and Jem hoped it wasn't a sign of things to come. He eyed Mel's black leather trousers and crop top sceptically. "Don't you have any doll's clothes you could put on or something?"

She scowled at him. "I've taken a warming tonic. I'll be fine. It's not like I had a whole wardrobe of miniature clothes ready on the off-chance a wayward familiar shrank me. I'm just glad the clothes I was wearing shrank with me," she muttered, as she ran her hands self-consciously over her outfit.

Jem shrugged and started down the driveway. His fur would keep him warm. If she wanted to take her chances with hypothermia, that was up to her. FFS couldn't blame him for that, could they?

The bus stop was a five-minute walk from Mel's house – or at least it would have been if it wasn't for the slowcoach witch travelling with him. More than once, he'd had to stop her from being blown down a sewer grate when a strong gust of wind caught her. The cracks in the pavement had also posed a slight obstacle, and she'd fallen on her face within minutes of leaving the house. Her terror when a pigeon had landed beside her was the highlight, however, and he'd had a good chuckle as he watched her run away screeching.

"The market will have moved again at the rate you're going," he said, stepping over her as she tripped yet again.

She climbed to her feet, brushing herself off. "I'm sorry that we're not all used to being such short-arses," she snapped.

As she stormed past, Jem couldn't help but think she'd make a very appealing chew toy. The thought reminded him how worryingly breakable she was, and he scanned their surroundings warily for any sign that there might be a dog nearby. It probably wouldn't do if she got herself eaten while they were on this little outing.

Irritated that he had to actually worry about her well-being now, he hurried to catch up with her. They'd just reached the main road when a crack of thunder sounded and the heavens opened in a deluge. Within seconds, his fur was soaked through, and Mel bore a remarkable resemblance to a purple-haired drowned rat.

She looked down at herself and gave a weary sigh as the rain teemed over her and splashed to the ground in fat droplets. Setting her mouth into a line of grim determination, she straightened up and marched on.

That odd little kernel of guilt niggled at him again, but he pushed it away. If she hadn't been trying to impress the covens with her stupid potion, they could be nice and warm at home right now. What self-respecting witch wanted to join a coven, anyway?

For as long as magic existed, witches and familiars worked together. It was the natural order. A witch of Mel's talent and potential didn't need to be subjugating herself to a bunch of old crones who thought they knew better. Maybe if she realised that, they wouldn't be in this mess.

The wind picked up as they trekked on, and the rain pelted them relentlessly. It didn't even work in their favour since the wind was blowing against the direction they needed to go, turning the simple walk into a nice, soggy workout. For Jem, it was an inconvenience that only served to make him grumpier. But for Mel, who wasn't yet used to her reduced body mass, it quickly became a physical impediment.

Given how slowly the witch was moving, they were likely to miss the bus, and there was no way Jem was staying out in this weather longer than he had to. With a huff of frustration, he moved behind her and used his head to push her onwards.

Mel's indignant protests carried to him on the wind, but he ignored her. They were making progress, and that was all that mattered. She could thank him later.

By the time the bus stop came into view, the wind had died down and the rain had shifted from fat droplets to a fine mist that was almost more annoying. An old lady and a harried mother with two young boys huddled under the bus shelter, hiding from the elements while they waited. It solved the problem of getting the bus to stop, at least, but it meant Jem and Mel would have to stay out of sight until it arrived.

Pushing her sodden hair back off her face, Mel gestured towards the row of bushes that ran behind the shelter. Silently, they made their way to the dense overgrowth, keeping a watchful eye on the waiting passengers.

*If anyone turns this way, lie down and play dead. I'll pretend you're my dolly,* he told her telepathically once they were settled beneath the dripping foliage.

The look she gave him would have been enough to cause a weaker familiar than he to wither, but he kept his innocent expression firmly in place. It was a perfectly reasonable suggestion.

The wait for the bus to arrive seemed never ending. When it finally pulled up at the bus stop with the squeal of brakes, Mel eagerly hurried forward.

Jem body-slammed her to halt her momentum, and she veered sideways into a small puddle. Her mouth dropped open in utter disbelief.

*Do you want the driver to see you?*

The stony silence that met his question was as good as a glowing commendation of his brilliance as far as he was concerned. He turned his attention back to the bus.

With a hiss, the door folded open. The two young boys ran forward only to be yanked back by the collars by their mother. She gave the old lady a haggard smile and motioned for her to board first.

Ever so slowly, the old woman hoisted herself up onto the low bus step. Only once she had flashed her bus pass at the driver and began her shuffle down the aisle did the mother release her brood. They barrelled onto the bus in a whirlwind of chaos.

*Come on.* Taking advantage of the distraction, Jem hurried for the door.

He cleared the distance between the path and the bus easily, and was quick to conceal himself behind the young mother while she rooted out change for bus fare.

Barely a second behind him, Mel leaped across the gap. She landed with an "oof" – her upper body in the bus, and her legs dangling in midair behind her. Clearly winded, she hung there, doing little else aside from clinging on while she attempted to get her breath back.

There was a hiss of hydraulics, and the door began to close.

Mel jerked her head up, eyes wide with panic. She scrambled, trying to find purchase on the smooth floor. Her face turned red as she hauled one knee up, but the second slipped on the rain-slick surface.

Rolling his eyes, Jem darted forward and grabbed the back of her top. He yanked her up just as the doors slammed closed.

*Come on.* Jem turned on his heel and followed the mother and her sons down the aisle. *Someone will see us if you keep lying there like you've been on the sauce all night.*

Looking somewhat pale, Mel picked herself up off the ground and followed him to the back of the bus.

The mother directed her two boys to the upper level and their argument over who got to sit next to the window drifted back down the stairs. Given the early hour, there were only a few other passengers scattered around the lower level, and they were too engrossed in their phones to notice the cat or his miniature human.

All except the old woman who'd gotten on at their stop.

As Jem passed her, she stared at him with rheumy eyes. There was no indication from her expression that she'd actually seen him, but something about those eyes made him shiver as he hurried on.

Once he and Mel had settled themselves safely out of sight in the footwell of the rearmost seats, Mel turned to him, her blue eyes blazing. "You could've helped a bit more," she hissed, jamming her fists on her hips.

He dismissed her anger with a snort. "You're on the bus, aren't you?"

"I was almost squashed!"

"Almost. But not quite."

She shook her head, dismay causing the fire in her eyes to bank. "You really don't care about anyone but yourself, do you?"

A sharp pain shot through him at her words. Brushing the feeling aside, he turned to settle in front of the air vent that was blowing warm, stale air into the bus, pointedly not meeting her eyes.

It didn't matter what she thought of him. They'd get this whole mess sorted, and he'd be out of her hair before long. She could go back to her normal life without the inconvenience of dealing with his self-ishness.

# CHAPTER ELEVEN

Jem inhaled deeply, letting the fresh air chase the stench of public transport from his nose. As much as it could, anyway. He was pretty sure his fur was going to permanently stink.

Next to him, Mel grimaced as she examined the underside of her shoe. He'd warned her to be careful where she was walking, but in her hurry not to miss their stop, she'd stepped straight into a glob of chewing gum on the bus floor. He'd yanked her free before the door closed and cut off their escape, but it had been close.

She sighed, giving up on the last tendrils that clung with stubborn determination. "Where to now?"

"This way." He ushered her towards the nearby corner, being careful to keep close to the looming grey buildings that lined the road.

Luck had been on their side that the old lady who'd

gotten on at the same stop as them also needed to get off at their stop. Her long skirt had provided convenient cover, and aside from Mel almost blowing it with the chewing gum fiasco, they'd gotten off the bus without drawing too much attention.

Oddly, the old lady had given Jem a knowing look before turning to walk in the opposite direction. He couldn't shake the feeling that she knew what they were up to, but he hadn't sensed a witch's aura from her, and since she'd left without causing any trouble, he pushed the thought away.

When they reached the corner, they turned left down a narrow side street. A large metal archway came into view at the end of it, and he could see a bustling market on the far side. As if a veil had been lifted, the calls of the market stall holders suddenly penetrated the quiet of the street.

"Fresh strawberries. Get your fresh strawberries."

"Wrapping paper, two for five euro."

Mel's brow scrunched in confusion. "This is just a normal market."

He gave her a blank look. "What did you expect? That the black market would be sitting here, visible to all and sundry?"

Her frown deepened and she shrugged. "Well, no. I guess not. I just figured it would hide somewhere less conspicuous than in a human market."

"What better place to hide than in plain sight?"

Steeling himself for the sickly-sweet smell of rotten fruit he knew was only going to get stronger, he started towards the archway. Mel kept close to his side and as they crossed through to the market, he herded her towards a stack of discarded cardboard boxes that were piled against the brick wall to their left.

From the cover afforded by the boxes, he had a clear view of the market. A double row of stalls formed a walkway leading to a large corrugated steel warehouse at the end. Customers milled about, moving in and out of the warehouse where more pointless goods no doubt awaited their attention. Thankfully, all were too caught up in the thrall of a potential bargain to look their way.

"Okay, let's get this over with," he said to Mel, trying his best to ignore the stench coming from the questionable puddle next to them. The quicker they got this done, the quicker they could be out of here.

Without waiting for a response, he extended his claws and made a small incision on the back of his paw.

Mel cringed, but held out her left arm for him to do the same to her. A quick swipe of his paw later and crimson liquid welled up from the neat red cut.

"Draw three parallel lines on the ground with the blood," he instructed as he dabbed his paw in his own blood.

He timed his final line so that it coincided with hers, and a sudden silence fell around them. The air shimmered, blurring his vision, and something slithered over his fur.

With a sharp *Pop!* everything snapped back into focus.

Night replaced day as the market sounds returned. This time, however, they were hushed and secretive as those who bartered sought to conceal their underhanded dealings. A full moon shone overhead, and its ambient glow mingled with the ethereal sparkle of the fairy lights that guided the way deeper into the market.

A glance back through the archway showed him that the narrow side street beyond the market was now gone. In its place was a gaping void of darkness. Of course, the street wasn't actually gone, but rather, hidden from view. The concealment spell that surrounded the black market ensured that it remained safely hidden from prying eyes ... and from witnesses.

Other than the sudden absence of daylight and questionable intentions of the patrons, the black market bore a remarkable resemblance to the human one. Stalls bordered either side of the pathway, their wares often not too dissimilar to the mundane counterpart.

Where there had moments ago been fruit and veg stalls, there now stood stalls displaying exotic plants and herbs such as wolfsbane and deadly nightshade. Jewellery stalls continued to offer pendants and trinkets, though now they held charms of protection – or harm – depending on the intention of the acquirer. Even the stall of children's toys remained. Only the Rubik's cube it sold would do more than simply perplex the user if the mischief curse it was advertised to contain was any indication.

This was the part of the market for the faint of heart lawbreakers. Those who wanted to acquire something not strictly legal, but that, in truth, caused no serious harm to procure or when used. It allowed them to flirt with the dark side, then run back home giggling to tell their friends how brave they'd been to dip their toe into the dark underbelly of the magical world. If they had any real idea what lay deeper in its depths, they'd run screaming.

Jem had no desire to dip his toe or anything else into this world. He'd been to the market when circumstances necessitated, but the black market was not a safe place for familiars – for anyone really, but familiars in particular – and his skin was already itching with the urge to get out of here.

He turned to Mel, who was still staring at their surroundings in awe – spot the newbie! "What's first on the list?"

She blinked as if suddenly remembering they were here for a reason. "Belladonna."

"That should be easy enough." He led the way into the market, keeping a wary eye on their surroundings as he did.

Many of the consumers mingling around the stalls were of the witch variety, though he spotted the occasional goblin, a dryad, and even a gorgon who being given a very wide berth despite the fact her snakes were safely ensconced in the silk scarf wound around her head. Some patrons had their features hidden within the shadowy hoods of cloaks and avoided eye contact with anyone around them, while others flaunted their illegal activity with a cocky air that pegged them immediately as novices to this world. He ignored them all, focusing only on their task.

As the stalls selling herbs and organic materials were the most abundant in this part of the market, they had their choice of sellers. He eyed the options, trying to gauge which would be the least treacherous to bargain with.

"Oh, look. This stall has some." Mel moved eagerly towards a stall on her right.

Jem snapped out a paw to stop her as a large leather boot stomped down next to her, splashing them both with mud and rainwater. "Watch where you're going. No one here is going to lose sleep if they accidentally squash you."

Looking slightly paler than she had a moment ago, Mel pointed a shaking hand to an innocuous-looking potted plant on the stall with dull green leaves and small black berries. "That's the belladonna we need."

Jem gave one look at the stallholder and kept walking. "Not this one."

He could sense the small winged woman watching Mel with keen eyes as the witch hurried to catch up with him.

"Why not that one?"

"You want to deal with a pixie? I didn't realise you were so eager to part with a vital organ ... or worse."

Pixies had used propaganda to their advantage for many centuries. People assumed because they were small, they were harmless, and pixies happily played on this stereotype to lure in unsuspecting prey. In truth, the little buggers were ruthless. They'd been known to flay a man alive simply for addressing them at a bad moment, and he had no desire to try and bargain with one.

Continuing to scan the stalls, Jem zeroed in on a tall man with a bulging forehead that showcased a single eye at its centre. "Here."

Mel's steps faltered as she took in the man's slightly green-tinged skin and hulking presence.

The stall was one of the quieter ones. Many of the shoppers stopped to glance at the array of herbs on offer, only to swiftly move on when they saw the creature manning it. An ogre or a cyclops would have been daunting for anyone to face, but a combination of both ensured this stall holder would struggle for business even here in the black market.

Jem nudged her with his head. *Ask him his price,* he instructed, switching to their mind-speak.

*Me?*

*Yes. You!*

He'd warned her before they left the house that money wasn't the currency of choice at the black market. Now, they'd see exactly how good her bartering skills were.

Swallowing hard, she looked from him to the stallholder and wiped her hands on her trousers. Some-what uncertainly, she edged forward.

"Excuse me," she said, looking up at the half cyclops, half ogre.

Her voice was drowned to nothing before it could reach the man's ears and he didn't even glance down.

"Eh, excuse me," she called, louder this time.

Still no response.

She looked helplessly at Jem, and he huffed. With a twitch of his nose, he lifted her up in the air so that she was flailing mid-air at eye level with the man.

"Eh, hi." She waved awkwardly before casting a furious glare back down at Jem. "How much for the belladonna, please?"

The cyclops ogre blinked in slow surprise, then grunted. "Your firstborn."

Mel's jaw dropped, and the man let out a loud guffaw, slapping the table and sending the potted herbs rattling around. "Newbies. Gets them every time."

She opened and closed her mouth, clearly at a loss for words. A frown replaced the shocked expression, and she jammed her fists on her hips, glowering.

Still laughing at his own hilarity, the stall owner took a moment to compose himself. Finally, he straightened up and wiped the tear from his eye.

"Sorry. I'm done. Promise. How much you need – the whole plant or just some leaves?"

"Five leaves and two ripe berries."

The cyclops ogre considered this. "Got any choco-late on ye?"

Once more taken aback, Mel patted her trousers. "Um, no?"

"You could promise to bring me back some."

Jem shook his head urgently. *No. Nothing that will force us to return.*

Mel straightened. "I'm afraid that won't be possible. Is there anything else you'd be willing to accept, or will I move to another vendor?"

The man scowled. "Fine. One hour of your life force, and it's yours."

Before Mel could react, Jem interjected. "Ten minutes."

"Thirty."

"Fifteen."

"Done."

The single large eye in the middle of the man's forehead glowed white, and the deal was done. With a smile, as if he hadn't just taken time from somebody's life, the stall holder neatly wrapped the leaves and berries and handed them to Mel.

# CHAPTER TWELVE

"I can't believe you gave away fifteen minutes of my life," Mel hissed. She jerked open the small pack affixed to Jem's back and shoved the pouch of herbs inside.

"Would you have preferred to give away your first-born? The cyclops might have been joking, but the pixie probably would have taken it. Be grateful a few measly minutes of your life was all you had to give up."

Mel growled, pulled the strap tight on the pack to secure it, and stomped off. Jem watched her go, irritated. A little gratitude wouldn't go astray here. And where exactly did she think she was going?

For a moment, a small part of him was tempted to let her find the remaining two ingredients by herself. He could find somewhere warm and dry to put his paws up while he waited. Of course, that would no doubt lead to her getting herself killed. So, grumbling to himself, he hurried after her, casting a wary eye around as he did.

"Where next?" Mel asked, keeping her gaze pointedly fixed ahead as he drew level with her.

He gestured with a paw towards the vast warehouse that loomed dark and foreboding ahead of them. It was a mirror image of the rusty, corrugated steel building that had been there in the human market, but deep shadows obscured the entrance to this one, and the very energy of the place made Jem want to turn and flee.

Given how highly he valued self-preservation, he was tempted to do just that, but the second ingredient on the list was a phoenix feather. It was an ingredient that was not only rare, but also dangerous to acquire, and there was no way they'd find one hanging around out here. He had no choice but to see this through, or self-preservation would take on a whole new meaning when FFS stripped him of his magic.

Next to him, Mel stared up at the building, her features pinched. She better not be getting cold feet.

"Try to keep up," he snapped, nerves making him edgy. "This isn't a place to take time for window-shopping."

She muttered a few choice words to herself, but stayed close to his side as they crossed the wall of shadows into the warehouse, leaving the pale light of the moon behind them.

A musty smell tickled Jem's nose as the gloom engulfed him, distorting his senses and temporarily blinding him. It took a moment for his pupils to enlarge and everything to snap back into focus, and he reached out to assure himself that Mel was still next to him.

Unlike the front part of the market, open stalls were few and far between in the vast space. Instead, the warehouse was a warren of small huts and makeshift "shops". Some made it clear by their decor exactly what they dealt in – jars of animal parts lining the windows, wind chimes made of voodoo dolls. Others were completely nondescript. If you didn't already know what they specialised in, then you had no business gracing their door. All had wards surrounding them to defer prying eyes from the questionable transactions being conducted within.

The patronage was also noticeably different in here. Most of the witches browsing the stalls outside looked like any other mundane human. But the use of darker magics changed a person. It stained their soul, and that stain manifested in physical ways. A wart here, a gnarled feature there. In the outside world, it was common to use glamours to conceal such telltale signs of dark magic use. Here, nobody bothered.

The percentage and variants of fae also increased significantly in this part of the market. The lure of power combined with a chance to hone their bargaining skills was too tempting to pass up and many enjoyed frequenting the market, both in a buyer and seller capacity.

Huddling close to him, Mel took in their surroundings with wide eyes. "How do we find a phoenix feather?"

"Look for dead animals."

She blanched in horror, a protest clearly on the tip of her tongue.

"Oh, relax," he interjected quickly before she got all emotional. "They wouldn't kill a phoenix for the feather. It will just help us find somebody who specialises in ingredients of animal origins."

Of course, there was every possibility that the phoenix might be killed for other parts, but he definitely wasn't going to point that out to her. Instead, he scanned the nearby shacks and took note of which might be an option for procuring their second ingredient.

If Mel was annoyed at the few measly minutes of her life he'd given away outside, she'd have an apoplexy at the haggling that went on in here. He'd have to find a vendor that played on the lower end of the evil scale – unless they wanted to play Russian roulette with their lives and try to steal the feather.

The idea was actually more than a little tempting, and Jem took a minute to imagine himself staging the heist of the century before snapping back to reality and urging Mel to get moving.

Thankfully, not too many people paid them any heed – the cat and the miniature human were far from the strangest thing gracing these four walls. Still, he kept them to the shadowy edges of the walkways as they moved. He didn't fancy ending up as a showpiece in one of the shop windows that displayed taxidermy animals, and flaunting the fact there was a familiar in their midst was a surefire way to guarantee trouble.

As they turned a corner, a withered old hag stepped into their path. Her eyes were milky white and her grey hair hung in scraggly clumps around her face. She bared teeth that were yellow and decaying as she pointed a gnarled finger at Mel.

"I see your future, child. Shall I tell you what awaits you?"

Jem rolled his eyes. Bloody fortune-tellers and their dramatics. They didn't have time for this crap. He stepped around the hag, not sparing her another glance lest she start spouting rubbish about his future too. "Come on," he said to Mel, who stood frozen on the spot in surprise.

"You seek their approval, but you shall not get it." The hag cackled. "There is no place in the covens for you."

There was a puff of smoke, and once more the space before them was empty.

Mel held a hand out, eyes wide and panicked. "Wait –"

"Mel," he snapped. "Forget the crazy lady and come on."

She turned to him, beseeching. "But she knows something about my coven application. I need to talk to her."

He shook his head in disgust. They were here to get the ingredients they needed to fix her, not to consult crystal balls. His magic was on the line, and she was worrying about her bloody coven application?

Well, screw this. She could stay here and risk being eaten by some nasty creature that fancied a pint-sized snack. He wasn't standing around all day.

He stalked off, making his way to the end of the winding path where yet another turn led deeper into the maze of shops. As he walked, he continued to scan for a potential vendor. He'd just gotten distracted by a questionable Christmas tree-like display made of skulls when a familiar figure caught his attention.

The old lady from the bus shuffled along, not fifty feet from where he stood. She seemed almost oblivious to her surroundings, but Jem knew nobody ended up in this place by accident. He hadn't sensed a magical aura from her before, but there had definitely been something odd about her. And now she was here.

Curiosity pricked at him despite his better judgement. He should really go back and fetch Mel – assuming she'd had enough time to get over her little snit – so they could hurry this whole thing along. Checking up on old Mother Hubbard wasn't really on the to-do list.

The old lady disappeared around a corner, and despite the little pep talk he'd just finished giving himself, he edged further down the path. He could see nothing beyond the end of the row besides dark shadows, and naturally, that piqued his curiosity even further.

Maybe he'd just have a quick look? It would only take a second. What harm would that do?

Before he could talk himself out of it, he hurried past the remaining shops and to the corner where the old lady had turned. A wall of impenetrable darkness met him, and he skidded to a stop, almost realising too late that it was an actual wall.

A flash of light came from his left, and once more he caught sight of the old lady. She stood in front of an open doorway, illuminated by a dull yellow glow. She turned to meet his eyes and gave him a knowing look. Then she disappeared through the opening.

Unease skittered over him as the door shut behind her and darkness once more reigned supreme. This was edging a bit close to that line between curiosity and dead cat even for him, so he turned back to find Mel and tell her to stop wasting time.

Electricity filled the air.

Then he felt it: the jolt of magic searing through him.

---

Unfamiliar voices pierced the veil of Jem's subconscious. For a moment he thought he'd overindulged in catnip again; then he remembered where he'd been before everything went black.

That goddamned helpless old lady had put a magical whammy on him!

Seething, he kept his eyes closed and opened his

senses. He pushed his magic outwards, seeking, probing. The tendrils made it only a couple of inches before they hit a barrier of some sort and fizzled out. He blinked his eyes open in surprise – and found himself staring at the bars of a cage.

The crackling blue aura around the bars suggested they were magically reinforced, but still he reached out a paw. He made contact with the one closest to him and was rewarded with a sharp zap of electricity. He jerked his paw back, grimacing at the stench of singed fur.

This was bad.

His view through the bars told him little about his surroundings. The room he was in was small, maybe eight feet by eight feet, with a single light bulb hanging limply from the ceiling. It did a poor job of illuminating the dank space, but given the grim sight, it was probably for the best.

More cages lined the walls, some empty, some containing shadowy figures that were curled in on themselves, making it impossible to tell what they were. There was no sign of the old lady – or anyone else for that matter – but the voices were close, just beyond the door of the small room.

He had no idea what she wanted with him, but it was unlikely to be anything good. He needed to get out of here. Now.

Once more, he reached out with his magic, methodically probing the cramped confines of his cell for any hint of weakness. There was none. The top, the bottom, all of it had been reinforced with magic. The large padlock that held the door closed was ideal for a little claw lock-picking, but it was tantalisingly out of reach on the other side of the magical aura.

That left him only one other choice. And didn't it damn well piss him off to admit it – even to himself.

Delving down deep inside, he reached for the bond that tied him to Mel. Though his head was still groggy from the magical concussion, he had a vague memory of walking off on her when she'd had a hissy fit over something or other related to the covens. He could only hope she wasn't in the mood to hold a grudge as he swallowed his pride and called to her.

Silence.

He tried again, but with the same result. He was either too far from Mel for their telepathic connection to work, or the magic that was protecting the bars was blocking that too.

The voices outside the door grew louder and, a moment later, the door cracked open. A woman's voice came from just beyond, her tone hard, brokering no argument.

"Get the familiar ready. The auction will start soon."

## CHAPTER THIRTEEN

A tall, lanky man in a starched black suit and glass monocle stepped up to the podium, and the buzz of excitement in the round chamber reached fever pitch. He held up his hand, and an instant hush fell around the room.

Dread solidified like cement in Jem's chest as he looked out through the bars of his cage. He'd heard rumours about these auctions before – rumours spread in hushed whispers that told of familiars disappearing never to be seen again. He was so screwed.

The auctioneer cleared his throat. "I believe many of you will agree when I say we have a very special treat for you today. A rare pedigree familiar – bred from Magdalena the First herself. Feast your eyes on the magical potential." He swept an arm out in a wide flourish and stepped aside to allow everyone a clear view of the cage. "Of course," he added with a wheezy rattle that might have been a chuckle, "what you do with that potential is your business."

A chorus of gasps and chilling "oohs" filled the space, and Jem felt the crushing weight of the hungry gazes that turned his way. He cowered back into the tiny cage and hissed.

Even in the gloom of the chamber, he could see that not all the faces were human. All were grotesque, however, the ravages of dark magic worn like a badge of pride here in the underbelly of the dark market. And all were here for him.

He couldn't see any sight of the old lady who had lured him here, but he had no doubt she had to be around somewhere. She was probably hiding in the shadows, cackling to herself, just waiting for the money to start rolling in.

The auctioneer proceeded to list Jem's attributes, beginning with his base measurements and then moving to the expected magical benefits – drastic power augmentation, elemental manipulation, potential for communing with the deceased.

Anticipation boiled over, and people began shouting bids from the crowd before the auctioneer had even declared the lot open for bidding.

Jem's mind raced as he desperately grasped for a way out of this mess. If he was given to one of these patrons, he was going to wish that FFS had stripped him of his magic. He'd be made a slave, unable to refuse a command from his "owner". And he didn't even want to think what kinds of things he'd be forced to do – things that even with his questionable conscience would give him nightmares.

Official bidding opened to a rather complimentary half a million.

Jem ignored those shouting numbers from the crowd, instead scanning his surroundings for exits. They'd covered his cage before bringing him to the auction chamber, but the downward trajectory had been obvious, so it stood to reason he was under the warehouse somewhere. The path had been winding and impossible to keep track of, but he'd damn well find his way... Assuming he could get out of this stupid cage.

His earlier tests of the bars had left him little hope of breaking out. That meant he'd have to wait until a winner was announced and they unlocked the cage to hand him over. It would leave him no margin for error, but he couldn't see any other choice.

The bidding price rose higher and higher.

As he desperately searched for a door, a window, or even a bloody vent, he spotted her. The old lady from the bus stood in a shadowy recess on the edge of the crowd. She observed the proceedings with a kindly smile on her face, and the irony of that expression almost made Jem puke in his mouth. He was going to wipe that smile off her face before he left here – old lady or not.

A sudden hush fell over the chamber.

Jem jerked his attention back to the crowd, his fur standing on end. A wave of power washed through the room, and the crowd undulated and parted down the centre. His instincts screeched a warning at him, but he could do nothing except stand and watch as a black-robed figure oozed forth from the shadows.

Darkness writhed with every move the figure made, and from within the deep cowled hood, two piercing green eyes fixed on Jem.

"Five million euro."

The voice was barely more than a whisper, a gentle breeze that drifted across the chamber. But it echoed inside Jem's head, reverberating in his very bones, in his soul. For the first time in a very long time, he was truly afraid.

Silently, he willed someone – anyone – else to bid, to save him from whatever this creature was. His pleas fell on deaf ears as the gavel slammed down on the podium.

"Sold!"

Unhappy murmurs rumbled through the chamber, but nobody dared voice their displeasure loud enough to draw attention to themselves.

Near paralysed with the terror that was trying very hard to choke him, Jem prepared himself. Somebody would come fetch him from the cage soon; he had to be ready. No matter what, he *had* to get out of here.

A loud *BOOM* echoed through the chamber, and the room erupted in a chorus of surprised yells. People scattered, some pulling magic to them as they did and casting the space in an eerie green glow.

*BOOM.*

Another explosion sounded on the far side of the room, and this time it was followed by a burst of colourful lights. Reds. Blues. Golds. They ricocheted around the room like someone was firing a rainbow-coloured machine gun.

Only it wasn't a machine gun, Jem realised as he watched the spectacle in stunned confusion. It was fireworks. A whole damn load of fireworks.

An ear-splitting screech sounded from the far corner of the room as a column of flame shot up towards the ceiling. The crowd became frenzied as half vied for the exits, while the rest sought the unseen foe, preparing to defend themselves.

Only one person remained steadfast in the chaos – the robed figure.

Jem could feel his new owner's eyes fix on him, their eerie green glow possessive within the shadowy cowl. The figure flowed against the panicked crowd, growing closer and closer with each second Jem stood frozen in fear. Trapped.

There was a sharp *Pop!* and a miniature rocket whizzed across the room. It zoomed past the robed figure's shoulder, a plume of purple smoke trailing in its wake. The smoke solidified and took the form of a huge, purple dragon.

People screamed as it dived into the crowd, bursting into smoke, only to reappear again a moment later somewhere else. Whatever calm remained was instantly shattered.

*Jem.*

Jem jerked his head around at the urgent whisper in his mind. His mouth dropped open in surprise.

Not more than five feet away, Mel peeked out from behind the curtain that hid pending auction lots from view. Her features were tight with tension, but her blue eyes shone with excitement. With some difficulty, she emerged from her hiding spot and began hauling something long and cumbersome towards his cage.

How in the name of Hecate had she gotten here?

Even as questions filled his head, he was able to make out the brass key she dragged behind her. Hope surged through him, but he tamped it down. The bars were warded; there was no way she'd be able to get him out.

He opened his mouth to warn her about the wards – lest she crispy-fry herself before she could be any use to him – but shut it again as she held a warning finger to her lips.

With an irritated growl, he silently warned, *The bars are warded.*

She ignored him.

Fine. Let her find out the hard way if that's what she wanted. He'd tried to tell her.

More mini explosions set his ears ringing, and he cast an anxious glance behind him, suddenly remembering both the robed figure and the dragon. There was no sign of either.

The chamber was filled with a purple haze from the smoke that had made up the ethereal creature, but the auction patrons were slowly realising that the threat held little true substance and order was return-ing. They were running out of time.

When he turned back to urge Mel to hurry, she was already hefting the large key from the ground. In her shrunken state it was almost as big as her, and she stumbled under the weight of it. Gritting her teeth in determination, she braced her feet and tried again to lift it.

The key raised unsteadily towards the lock, and Jem held his breath.

The blue aura surrounding the bars flickered as the key made contact with the metal. But there was no spark, and no yelp of pain from Mel. The witch shot up a few notches in his esteem.

Had she found some way to circumvent the ward, or was the key simply that – the key to it? Unable to help himself, Jem reached out a tentative paw to touch the door of the cage. He jerked back at the jolt of now-familiar pain and scowled at the stench of burning fur.

Mel raised her eyebrows in disbelief. *Are you quite done?*

He didn't bother answering, just moved back to keep clear of the bars while she worked the key into the lock. After some wriggling and grunting, there was a soft click. The door swung open, and Jem wasted no time in leaping for blessed freedom.

"Order!" the auctioneer called over the room. "Order!"

Silence fell, punctuated by a pop and fizz as one final firework was snuffed out. Jem met Mel's wide-eyed look with one of his own as all eyes in the room turned back towards the stage.

"Run," he urged, forgetting to use his quiet voice as the need to flee spurred him into motion.

Surprised yells sounded as he herded her back to the curtain at the rear of the stage. The gloom swallowed them whole, and his eyes instantly sharpened their focus to compensate.

Cages and crates loomed before them, forming an obstacle course they had no choice but to navigate. It slowed their progress significantly, and footfalls sounded behind them within seconds. It was only a matter of time before somebody caught up to them.

Jem increased his speed but was soon outpacing Mel's shortened stride length. Growling in frustration, he sent out a burst of magic. She winked out of existence, and a second later, her weight settled onto his back.

*Tell me where to go*, he ordered, ignoring her surprised yelp.

Grasping his fur tightly, she jabbed a finger towards the left-hand corner of the room. There was no exit that Jem could see, but the angry voices were growing closer by the second, so he bit back his protest, and did as instructed.

A solid wall loomed out of the darkness before him. He skidded, trying to halt his momentum, but instead of crashing into it, they passed straight through the wall and slid to a stop on the other side.

Confused, Jem took in the narrow tunnel where

they now stood. The walls, floor, and ceiling were hard packed mud, and the air was thick and cloying. The darkness was so complete that even his eyes struggled to adapt this time.

"Where –"

Mel gave his fur a sharp tug, halting the question he'd accidentally asked out loud.

*Shh,* she warned. *They'll hear you.*

As if summoned by her words, the voices that had been haunting their retreat grew louder. Jem looked out from the tunnel as the auctioneer stepped around the curtain. The old lady from the bus followed in his stead and scanned the space with beady eyes full of sharp cunning.

"Find them," she demanded.

The auctioneer nodded and moved into the room, methodically making his way through the maze of crates and cages. He placed a hand on top of each he passed, blue magic sparking from his fingertips. Low whines and screeches of pain filled the air.

Jem's heart thundered in his chest, and he edged backwards, preparing to bolt.

Mel placed a steadying hand on the back of his neck. *Wait. Don't move.*

*We need to go.*

*Trust me.* She ran her hand down his fur, her touch gentle.

Her calm surety trickled down the bond, and he suddenly realised that their connection was back. The unnatural silence that had met him when he'd reached out to her from within the cage was gone, replaced now with a vibrant buzzing that both comforted him and left him feeling oddly exposed.

Despite his every instinct demanding he run, Jem decided to trust her. She'd found him in this hellhole against all odds, so maybe she knew something he didn't. He had to hope that she was right and their hiding spot was safe, otherwise they'd have lost any chance of a head start.

Keeping perfectly still, Jem allowed his claws to extend. The auctioneer might have magic, but a claw to the crown jewels would be a pretty surefire distraction if the man tried to weave any nasty spells.

As the auctioneer reached the cage closest to them, Jem felt Mel tense on his back. His resolve to trust her wavered, and he prepared himself to run.

The man turned to the darkened corner where they stood playing statues. He tilted his head and adjusted the monocle that covered his left eye.

This was it. They were done for.

Jem's tail twitched, and his muscles tensed, screaming to act.

The man reached out a hand, staring intently at them, but not showing any hint that he'd seen them. His fingers came within an inch of Jem's fur.

The curtain blocking off the stage was yanked back. A shadowy form flowed into the room, and the auctioneer blinked, jerking back as his concentration was broken.

"Where's my familiar?"

The whispered voice filled Jem's head and sent an icy chill slithering through him. His muscles locked with fear, and he was no longer frozen to the spot of his own choice.

The old lady slowly turned to face the robed figure, wariness evident in the sudden stiffening of her frame. "Xyanthia. Apologies for this inconvenience. We will have this ... situation rectified shortly."

"See that you do. Or I will rase this market to the ground."

## CHAPTER FOURTEEN

I t took some quiet words and solemn oaths from the old lady that the familiar would be found, but eventually, the robed figure left the rear of the stage with her. The auctioneer hesitated for a moment longer, his attention once more flicking to the dark corner where Jem stood frozen in the tunnel with Mel on his back. He frowned, but turned to follow his companions.

Jem slumped to the earthen floor, his legs somewhat shaky. The echo of that *thing's* voice stayed with him even though he could no longer see the robed figure, and a shiver ran through him that had nothing to do with the atmospheric temperature.

Mel clambered off his back and turned towards the welcoming blackness of the tunnel. *We need to get going.*

Forcing himself to pull it together, Jem nodded and rose to his feet. On silent paws, he followed her into the narrow space that his mind still insisted shouldn't be there.

Little changed within the tunnel as they left the auction chamber behind and began the upward trajectory that would hopefully lead them back to a safer part of the market. The musty smell of packed earth tickled Jem's nose, and even his eyes struggled with the complete lack of light. He kept close to Mel, ensuring he had contact with her at all times.

"How did you find this place?" he asked once he was sure it was safe to speak aloud again.

"Well, after you stormed off, I didn't have much choice other than to follow. I'd only just caught up as that creepy old lady was dragging you through the doorway, so I sneaked through after her. From what I can tell, the whole underground of the market is a maze of hidden passages. They're obscured with spells, but not impossible to find. Once I knew what I was looking for, it was easy enough to use them to track you."

"But how did you not get caught?" He hadn't really pegged her as the stealthy ninja tracker type.

He sensed more than saw her frown at the obvious disbelief in his tone. But it was a fair question. He'd brought her to the black market expecting to be the one rescuing her, not the other way around.

"I used a distraction rune to encourage people not to look my way. And it turns out most people are too self-absorbed to take the time to look down anyway."

"And the fireworks? Where in the name of Hecate did you get them?"

"I, eh, may have borrowed them from one of the stalls."

Jem groaned, wondering how many people they'd have after them before they got out of this place. The thought made him cranky as he tried to ignore the lingering fear that his new "owner" was out there searching for him.

"You could've gotten me out sooner," he muttered, knowing it was unfair but needing to focus his fear on something.

"The room they held you in was heavily guarded. I had no chance of getting close. Besides, I needed the time to come up with a plan. Do you think they were going to let me simply waltz up and take you back?"

Time. His steps faltered as another thought occurred to him.

"How long was I down there for?"

Mel glanced sideways at him, and though he couldn't see her expression clearly, he already knew before she responded that he wouldn't like the answer.

"A few hours. It's early evening now."

"Shit."

"Yeah. We need to get the other two ingredients and get out of here before you get yourself into any more trouble." And before the inspector woke up.

Jem glowered at her back as she increased her pace. The witch was never going to let him forget that she'd saved him.

Putting the rest of his questions aside for now, he hurried to catch up with her. The air seemed to get fresher the further they went, and finally, a sliver of light appeared ahead. He broke into a run, the lure of freedom a beacon he couldn't ignore.

They came to a halt at what appeared to be boards of wood hammered haphazardly over an opening that separated the tunnel from whatever lay beyond. A low hum of voices came from the far side, warning that there were people nearby.

Carefully, Jem nudged the bottom board with his paw. It gave slightly at his touch, but some investigation showed a couple of rusty nails holding it in place. His claws made short work of those, and he only just caught the board before it hit the ground with a thud.

He crouched down and peered through the newly made opening to what appeared to be a loading bay at the rear of the warehouse. A raised metal shutter on the far side allowed a glimpse of the night sky. Though the moon was a constant here at the black market, it seemed to mock him now with the reminder that time was ticking away.

Rusted shipping containers lined one side of the large, square room, while stacked pallets containing boxes of Hecate knew what lined the other. A freight truck was parked in the centre of the space, its rear doors open and a loud crash sounded from within.

"Agh! Stupid bloody bird." The string of curses that followed would've been enough to make even Jem blush – if he was capable of doing so.

At his side, Mel scrunched her nose as an acrid smell drifted on the wind to them. *What in the name of –*

Her words cut off abruptly in his mind as two men approached the truck. They were broad, solid walls of muscle, and both had ginger hair with matching stubble covering their jaws. Even from a distance, a menacing air oozed from them, the type that no doubt made people clear a path for them wherever they went.

*Leprechauns.* Jem let a low hiss as his fur stood on end.

He hadn't encountered many in his life, but leprechauns were nothing like the cute little guys the human media believed them to be. They were mercenaries, willing to do almost anything – for the right price. And they were feared for good reason.

If they were here to take control of that shipment, then there was likely something very valuable inside. Something very valuable and very illegal.

Mel crouched down next to him as she, too, watched the men disappear inside the truck. *We should get out of here.*

It would be the clever thing to do, of course, but Jem's kitty senses were telling him to stay put. Unlike with his earlier curiosity where he'd known deep down it was going to get him in trouble, this was a more instinctual feeling, his magic trying to tell him something important. So, he stayed where he was, careful not to move or make a sound.

The two leprechauns appeared a couple of minutes later, carrying a large gold box between them as if it weighed nothing. Long, flame-coloured feathers protruded from a narrow slit in the side of the box.

Mel tugged on his fur with barely contained urgency. *Is that a...*

*Phoenix*, he confirmed, grimacing. If the bird was being guarded by two leprechauns, they had no hope of getting near it.

*We have to follow them.*

Mel moved to do just that, crouching down to slide under the opening he'd made in the wooden boards. When he didn't immediately follow, she turned back to him, eyebrows raised in question.

*Maybe we can find another supplier?* he suggested, aiming for casual nonchalance.

She folded her arms, shrewd blue eyes pinning him to the spot. *You're scared.*

*Am not.*

*Are too.*

He huffed. *Fine. Let's go get ourselves crushed to a bloody pulp by leprechauns.*

He stalked past her, ignoring her satisfied smirk. Not stupid enough to brazenly follow the two jacked-up Lucky Charm wannabees, he kept carefully to the edges of the loading bay, ensuring Mel was by his side.

The loading bay wasn't much larger than what they'd seen from their previous vantage point in the tunnel, and it wasn't long before they rejoined the hustle and bustle of the market. As soon as the leprechauns left the delivery area, they activated their magic and disappeared from sight in a quick burst of rainbow-coloured light.

Jem locked in on their scent, working hard to block out the other odours and noises of the market as he tracked them through the warren of shops. As he moved, he kept a wary eye on their surroundings, waiting for the robed figure or old lady to jump out at him at any moment. More than once he narrowly avoided being stepped on in his distraction.

Mel, on the other hand, seemed to have become infinitely more adept at staying out of the way of potential squash hazards. He found himself impressed at how she was adapting to her reduced size. Maybe she could just embrace the new look and they could go home?

The leprechaun's trail followed a winding pattern through the market that Jem could only assume was meant to throw off any attention. It finally came to a stop at a purple and blue stretch tent that was enclosed on all sides and looked like it could easily house a mini circus.

Mel glanced from it to him uncertainly. *Are you sure they went this way? That place doesn't exactly seem fireproof enough to hold a phoenix.*

He gave her a blank look in return, not deigning to answer.

And just to prove how idiotic she was for questioning his superior senses, voices drifted from the tent. A moment later, the two leprechauns pushed aside an opening in the colourful structure and stepped out, their precious cargo noticeably missing.

A statuesque woman with sleek blonde hair followed behind them. Her white pantsuit screamed money, and her strange smoky purple aura screamed danger.

"All seems to be in order with the delivery," she said to the leprechauns, her voice like rich honey.

Despite the soothing tone, Jem shivered. He'd only seen an aura like that once before. And it did not bode well for them.

The taller of the leprechauns grunted. "Did you expect any less?"

"Of course not." The woman placed a reassuring hand on his arm and gave him a wide smile that failed to thaw the cold calculation in her eyes.

He glared at the hand until she – wisely – removed it. "We'll take our payment now."

She made a moue of disappointment but reached into a pocket at the waist of her coat. When she pulled it back out, she held a small vial in her hands. The contents glittered gold and both leprechauns' gazes locked on it, enthralled.

"I believe that concludes our business, gentlemen?"

The two nodded silently, never taking their eyes from the glittering gold liquid. As one, they turned and disappeared back into the market. The woman watched them go with a satisfied smile.

*We need to get that feather,* Mel said as the woman

disappeared back inside, the tent opening falling closed behind her.

*She's not the type of person you want to bargain with.* Jem's tail drooped, and he wrapped it around himself protectively. *She's a sorceress.*

Mel sucked in a breath, clearly familiar with the lethal reputation that had been well-earned by the dark magic users.

Jem considered their options. The longer it took them to find a supplier, the higher the chances he'd be found by someone who wanted to use him as a magical puppet. Maybe if they could get the woman out of her tent...

*Don't suppose you've any more of those fireworks hiding somewhere handy?* As he asked, he eyed Mel's tiny frame and wondered how exactly she'd gotten the things down to the underground chamber in the first place. This witch really was a curiosity.

*Nope.* She was silent for a long minute as she chewed her lip. Suddenly, her eyes widened. *But I do have an idea.*

Jem took a wary step back. He didn't like that mischievous glint in her eye. Not one little bit. *What idea?*

*Okay, hear me out. Those people downstairs were bidding on you, weren't they?*

He nodded slowly.

*So, familiars are in high demand here.*

She was not going to suggest what he thought she was going to suggest... Was she?

*And it's a pretty safe bet that the woman in the tent likes to collect exotic animals, if the phoenix is anything to go by.*

He gave her his best killer kitty glare. *What exactly is your point?*

Her wide smile left no doubt in his mind what she was suggesting.

He thought of a myriad of arguments as to why it was a bad idea – the fact he'd only just escaped familiar enslavement being one pretty damn big one. But they needed that phoenix feather, and he couldn't think of another way that would get them one quickly.

Apparently noticing his resolve waver, Mel pushed her advantage. *All you have to do is keep her busy for a few minutes while I sneak in to get a feather. Obviously, you're smart enough to make sure she doesn't catch you.*

He knew she was buttering him up, but still he preened. He was pretty smart, and it wasn't too often a witch gave him express permission to get up to mischief. It would be a shame to pass up the opportunity.

*Fine. But be quick about it.*

Mel crossed her heart solemnly.

Now, if he was going to do this, he might as well make it fun.

# CHAPTER FIFTEEN

J em crept to the edge of the tent, listening for any sign of movement inside. He'd had a quick scout around the circumference of the structure and already identified the weak points. He might have also nicked one of the guide ropes with his claws, leaving it hanging together by a few tenuous threads.

He looked back to the corner where Mel waited in the shadows. The bond thrummed at his centre, and through it he could sense her nerves, despite the confidence with which she'd put forward her plan.

She was right to be nervous. Nobody really knew the true extent of a sorceress's power. They were a small faction of the magical community and had made it their business to keep their nature shrouded in mystery. One thing could be guaranteed, however – the woman inside the tent was powerful and dangerous, and it was a terrible idea to mess with her.

Crouching low, Jem edged towards the opening the leprechauns had emerged from. He steeled himself to run even as he ducked his head under.

The interior of the tent was a wide open space. Colourful carpets covered the floor, and cushions were scattered throughout. It looked almost like one of those places people went to meditate – which was just code for have a nap as far as he was concerned. The aroma of incense tickled his nose, heightening the association even further.

Of course, most meditation spaces didn't have a phoenix trapped in a golden box, resting on a stone podium at its centre. They also didn't have a crazy ass blonde businesswoman arranging what looked like animal bones around a pile of crystals at the podium's base.

It looked like she was setting a temporary ward, which meant she was likely planning to move the bird very soon. Even with the power he could feel emanating from her magic, he didn't think she'd be likely to leave an asset this valuable behind a makeshift ward for long. Not in a place like this, where most people – or creatures – you met were just waiting for a chance to sink their claws into you.

*Mel,* he called, hoping they hadn't overstretched the lengths of their telepathic connection. *The woman is putting a temporary ward on the bird. It's a strong one, but it's physical. I'll weaken the structure. Can you break the remaining threads of magic yourself?*

*Yes.*

He took the surety of her response at face value, gave himself a moment to assess the layout, then darted into the tent.

The bone and crystal arrangement at the base of the pedestal was his target. Without the freedom to work at leisure, he wouldn't be able to disable the ward entirely, but he could disrupt its energy flow to make it easier for Mel to do the rest.

The sorceress was placing a final bone into position when he zoomed right under her nose. There was a satisfying clatter of bones and a hiss, but that was all he had time to register before she was on his tail.

Despite the fancy stiletto shoes she wore, the sorceress moved quickly. More than once, a terrifyingly pointy heel stamped down a hair's breadth from his tail.

Jem covered a full circumference of the space to ensure she continued to follow him – and why wouldn't she? He was a pedigree familiar. Then, once he was certain her attention was on him alone, he squirrelled under the side of the tent right next to the guide rope he'd compromised earlier.

A hand snapped out after him, but he slipped free of its grasp as the sorceress flung the side open. He stood just out of reach, waiting for her to emerge fully. Then gave her his widest kitty grin.

And slashed the final threads on the guide rope.

The side of the tent next to the sorceress sagged inwards without the rope's tension, and she screeched.

Her beautiful face twisted and contorted in rage as she turned blazing purple eyes on him.

That was when she began chanting.

Power skittered over Jem's fur like an army of ants swarming him. He fought against the urge to unsheathe his claws and scratch his skin raw.

Her words built in power, and he knew he didn't want to be standing there when she finished. He turned and ran deeper into the market, praying to Hecate he could lose her in the maze.

The sorceress followed, not once breaking the rhythm of her chant. Market patrons veered out of their paths, clearly not wanting to be in the firing line for whatever drama was unfolding.

Jem moved in a zigzag pattern, eyes scanning his surroundings as he did. How long did Mel need to get the feather? He had to make sure the sorceress stayed away for long enough, or they wouldn't get a second shot at it.

A small shop at the end of the row caught his attention, the simple blackboard outside advertising it as a potions specialist.

Familiar magic didn't require the use of potions or magical paraphernalia to work; it was as instinctual as breathing. But that didn't mean they couldn't be useful. He'd gotten up to enough mischief in his time living with witches to know the potential of potions. And the dangers.

A crackle of electricity in the air warned him the sorceress was almost done casting whatever nasty curse she had planned. He threw a panicked glance over his shoulder and made a swift beeline for the potions shop.

Even here in the black market, potion safety was afforded the utmost respect and it was likely the truly volatile potions would be held within carefully spelled containers to prevent accidental – or intentional – breakages. Luckily for him, he knew exactly how unstable mundane ingredients could be too. His previous witch could attest to that.

There was no time to stop and search for what he needed, so he had to rely solely on his magic and his intention. He pictured the pink crystals his last witch had used to create a super-strength stain remover, and sent tendrils of his magic out, seeking.

For a second, the magic searched fruitlessly, not latching onto anything. The sorceress's voice reached a crescendo, and adrenaline shot through him.

Just as he prepared to dive out of the way, his magic locked onto its target. With a desperate burst of power, he called the crystals to him and sent another tendril out to grab one of the bottles of ammonia stacked inside the door.

He flung them both into the sorceress's path.

The ingredients were still in the air when the sorceress screeched her final word and released her curse. An eerie silence fell as time fractured.

Then her power hit the projectiles, and everything exploded.

Jem went flying through the air. He smashed into a

pile of wooden crates stacked a couple of shops down from where he'd been standing. Scrambling to untangle himself from the shattered wood, he jumped to his feet and hissed as pain shot through his side and back paw.

The place was in chaos. One side of the makeshift shop was scorched, and a gaping hole allowed a clear view of the damage inside. Cloying pink smoke filled the space, and people were running around frantically trying to put out the remnants of sparkly pink flames.

A squat, balding man emerged from the potions shop, coughing and spluttering, his red face suggesting his blood pressure was nearing heart attack levels. He zeroed in on the sorceress, who was rising slowly to her feet and looking murderous.

"What did you do to my shop?" the man yelled, shaking a fist at her.

Jem didn't stick around to see if she turned the man into a toad. He high-tailed it out of there, using her distraction to skirt around the side of the shops and out of sight. Still limping slightly, he wound a circuitous route back towards the sorceress's tent.

Mel wasn't at their agreed rendezvous point, and he had to stifle the panicked thought that maybe the sorceress had somehow returned and caught her.

*Mel?* he called silently.

*Inside.*

Jem frowned at the structure that was now looking a little more unstable thanks to his foray with the guide rope. Had she run into problems with the ward? He'd scattered the bones pretty well, so it should have been easy enough for her to finish the job.

Unless the sorceress had backup protections in place that he'd missed?

Conscious that the woman would likely be heading back this way very soon, he hurried to the tent and wriggled under the siding. He found Mel inside, staring at the gold box on the pedestal. She held a small flame-coloured feather in her left hand, and he could see absolutely no reason why she was still standing there.

"What are you doing? She'll be back any minute," he snapped. His side was aching after his run back to the tent, and the last thing they needed was another run-in with the sorceress.

Mel turned to him with a pained expression. "We need to free it. We can't leave it here."

It?

Realisation dawned on him, followed immediately by disbelief. She wanted to free the phoenix?

"We can, and we will. Now, let's go." He turned to leave, in no humour to argue.

"It's cruel. No animal should be left locked up in a box like this to be used for parts."

Jem's mind flashed back to that horrid cage, and to the robed figure who was no doubt out there looking for him as they stood here. Irritation flared through him. Of course no creature deserved that. But if Mel didn't get her arse in gear, they'd both find themselves locked up in a box right next to the phoenix – and that was if they were lucky.

"How do you think your precious coven sources their ingredients?" he said. It was a low blow, but this wasn't the time for her to get a conscience about what went on here in the market.

Her jaw tightened, but he didn't miss the flash of uncertainty in her eyes.

"They only use cruelty-free supply chains."

"Sure they do."

He turned to leave. She wasn't stupid enough to risk staying here; she'd see sense.

"I saved you from that auction. And now you won't help me?"

Her words stopped him cold.

So, that was it. She'd only saved him so she could hold it over him later. Had she even cared if anything happened to him?

A heavy lump settled in his throat as he realised that he'd actually started to let his guard down with her. With a self-deprecating laugh, he stalked from the tent and didn't look back.

# CHAPTER SIXTEEN

He was such a fucking idiot. He'd done the one thing he'd sworn never to do again – trusted a witch.

Why had he thought Mel would be any different? Yes, she might have agreed to come here instead of ratting him out straight away to FFS, but clearly she'd just been humouring him. When it came down to it, she would always choose what was best for her. If he was collateral damage as a result, then so be it.

Seething, he worked to put as much distance between himself and the tent as his aching side and paw would allow. If Mel wanted to spend her life as a magical Barbie doll, that was up to her. He was getting out of this damned place and FFS could have his bloody powers. At least then he wouldn't have to be stuck babysitting idiotic witches anymore.

Oddly cheered by the thought, he paused to take

stock of his location and pinpoint the exit. A loud *WHOOSH* sounded behind him.

He jerked around in time to see a huge white fireball shoot up into the air and through the ceiling of the warehouse.

Debris rained down, and people shrieked, scattering every which way. Jem stared at the chaos in fascination. Then it registered with him where the fireball had come from.

The centre of the warehouse.

The tent.

Mel!

Before he could even think about what he was doing, he was racing back in the direction he'd just come from. The chaos only intensified the closer he got – patrons fled, coughing and spluttering for the exits, while vendors packed up their wares or were busy casting spells of protection to avoid their stuff getting damaged.

The smoke reached him only a moment before he saw the flames. White hot and alive, they licked at the horizon, reaching up for the night sky now visible through the hole in the roof.

Jem rounded the bend and skidded to a stop.

He stared at the spot where the tent had been. Only now he could see straight across the warehouse, his view unhindered by the purple and blue structure. Because the tent had completely collapsed in on itself.

That same white flame he'd seen from a distance was an inferno in the middle of the collapsed tent, and though fireproofing spells were clearly trying to stop the spread, they were no match for the phoenix flame.

Struggling not to choke on the acrid smoke, he circled the structure. There was no sign of Mel.

*MEL,* he called, reaching out through the bond.

The only response was an urgent tug at the centre of his chest. His heart hammered, and he fought to keep calm; he had to think clearly.

It was easy enough to pinpoint from the scorching fire and hole in the ceiling where the phoenix had burst from the tent. Mel would have been close to that point in order to free the bird, but would she have had time to put space between them before the bird erupted?

Cursing the witch for her bleeding heart that was likely going to get her – and him – killed, he ran for the edge of the tent.

The flames were quickly spreading outwards from the centre and would soon consume the whole tent. If she was still under there, he had minutes at best to get her out.

Darkness enveloped him as he squirrelled under the heavy material. Even from here, the heat from the fire was like a tangible force. It seared his eyes and throat and, try as he might to surround himself with a protective bubble of magic, the phoenix flame was too strong. He closed his eyes and let instinct guide him.

The weight of the tent pressed down on him as he turned his focus inward to the bond that tethered him to Mel. The tug at the centre of his chest grew more urgent as he moved forward, but the bond flickered erratically. He had to hurry.

Something long and solid blocked the way in front of him, and he was forced to stop and blink his eyes open. Tears instantly blurred his vision as once more the soft tissues of his eyes were assaulted by the blinding heat.

From what he could make out in the darkness, it appeared to be one of the poles that had supported the interior of the structure while it stood. He edged along it, continuing his game of hot and scalding with the bond until he came to another solid object caught beneath the pole.

Only, it wasn't an object. It was Mel's prone form.

The metallic scent of blood filled Jem's nose, but he ignored it, focusing only on the pulse of the bond that told him she was alive. He nudged her with his nose, but there was no response.

Refusing to let panic take hold, he wriggled his body under the pole, placing himself between the hard metal and Mel's softer form. He gave a push of magic to take some of the weight away. It moved – barely – and with great effort, he manoeuvred her out from beneath it.

Sweat ran in rivulets down his fur, and it was clear from the blistering heat that the flames were growing ever closer. The constant weight of the tent was crushing, and it was all he could do to keep it from smothering Mel while he used a combination of his fatiguing magic and physical pushing to roll her back towards the edge.

He had no doubt she'd be cursing him for the bumps and bruises when she woke up, but she would wake up, dammit. How else was he going to say "I told you so"?

The moment they emerged from beneath the fabric was one of the greatest moments of relief Jem had ever experienced. He was exhausted and aching, and though he knew he still needed to get them clear from the raging fire and suffocating smoke, he instantly felt lighter and more able to breathe.

That newfound lease on life revived his magic just enough to allow him to lift Mel's still unconscious form and move her around the corner to a shadowy spot out of sight.

Behind them, market workers had surrounded the tent and were working to get the phoenix fire under control. Potions flew through the air, exploding into balls of water, and elemental fae had formed a line and were simultaneously siphoning off the flames. He ignored it all, focusing only on Mel as he laid her gently on the ground.

Black soot coated her face, and the rise and fall of her chest was shallow. Something twisted uncomfortably at his centre as he watched her closed eyes, waiting for them to blink open.

When they didn't, he nudged her with his paw. Nothing.

He slapped her cheek. Still nothing.

He nuzzled that same spot with his nose, then overcome with a sudden urge to clean the dirt from her, he licked the side of her face.

As he carefully worked around the cuts and grazes that marred her forehead, he focused on the bond that connected him to her and directed his energy through it. The human body was too complex for even the most experienced witch or familiar to magically heal much aside from the most basic of damage. But the body was also capable of its own magic, and with the right resources, could heal itself.

He would give Mel those resources, and she would wake the hell up, or he was going to go home and shred all of her furniture.

On his third lick, she stirred and cringed away from him. The movement sent her into a coughing fit that wracked her body. Eventually, it subsided and she blinked her red-rimmed eyes open.

"Jem?" Her voice was rough and sounded like she'd smoked fifty cigarettes a day her entire life. "What happened?"

"I told you to leave the bird, you silly witch." His earlier frustration at her melted away as relief filled him. She was alive. She'd be okay.

"Couldn't," she croaked. "Not right."

He shook his head but refrained from pointing out that way of thinking had almost gotten her killed. Of course, he supposed it was also the reason she'd saved him, so maybe he should cut her a bit of slack.

"Did you at least manage to hold on to the feather before you set the whole place on fire?"

Her eyes widened in momentary panic. She pushed up to sitting, triggering yet another coughing fit, and patted her trousers. After a moment, she pulled the top of a broken feather out of her back pocket.

Jem eyed what was left of the phoenix's plumage sceptically. "Will it be enough?"

She cringed. "Let's hope so."

"In that case, stop lying down on the job. We have one last ingredient still to get."

Mel scowled, but she clambered to her feet with only a little difficulty. She looked around, assessing their surroundings. "Any idea who might supply dragon heart stones?"

He gave a weary sigh, thinking of the warm cat bed that was waiting for him at home, Mr. Fluffles ready to be cuddled. "Unfortunately, yes."

An expectant pause forced him to utter the words he'd hoped never to have to say.

"We need a demon."

## CHAPTER SEVENTEEN

"And you're sure there's no one other than a demon who would have a dragon heart stone?"

Mel trudged along beside him, her complexion still a worrying shade of pale beneath the smudges of dirt. She had only grown paler when he told her what they'd need to do to get the third and final ingredient.

"Can you think of any other creature that would be willing to brave the depths of a volcano to acquire them?" He swore and darted to the side as a giant, lumbering man stomped past, almost turning Jem's tail into a pancake as he beat a hasty path to the exit.

"No, but..." She trailed off, her shoulders slumping in defeat.

He didn't blame her; the last thing he wanted to do was try bargaining with a demon – particularly one who made their living in the dark market. Demons were not inherently evil, despite common belief. But they were tricky as hell, and the payment for what they were after would be steep.

Lapsing into silence, they followed a winding path to the far left of the warehouse. Jem kept his eyes peeled as they went, occasionally scaling stacks of boxes or crates for a better view. The prickle of his fur was telling him they were being followed, and it was making him uneasy.

There was only one demon operating in the market that he knew was guaranteed to have the stone they needed. Var was well known for acquiring artefacts and ingredients that could be found in places many dared not go. He also had a reputation as a shrewd business-man, and wouldn't have been Jem's first choice to approach if they'd had more time.

The demon's "shop" couldn't have looked any more out of place in the market if it tried. On a raised plat-form so it looked over the surrounding shops, the glass-fronted structure looked more suited to a high-end boardroom. Magic coated the glass, making it impossible to see inside from where they stood, but Jem could easily picture Var sitting on a throne, looking out at all those he believed beneath him.

The few patrons that remained in this part of the market gave the shop a wide berth, and as he and Mel traversed the path to their destination, he wished he could do the same.

Jem didn't wait for Mel to ask for help; he floated her up the metal steps that led to a solid black door. As he bounded up the steps after her, the door swung open and a deep, velvety voice called, "Please, do come in."

Mel gave Jem a wary look that matched his own feelings, but he held his head up high as he marched inside.

Sure enough, as the exterior had suggested, Jem found himself in what could only be considered a boardroom – or the office of a CEO who required large things to compensate for other areas that were lacking. Rich wood panelling complemented the wall of glass that did indeed provide a clear view out, and a large round table was surrounded with black leather chairs, all of which were currently empty.

Beyond that, two leather sofas faced each other with a glass coffee table in between. The demon reclined on one of the sofas, watching them, a glass tumbler filled with rich amber liquid in hand.

Var was every inch the business executive in his finely tailored charcoal suit and black shirt. He was pretty boy good-looking with his black hair and bright silver eyes, but beneath his wide smile was a sly cunning, and sharp teeth just waiting to snap closed on them.

"Jeremiah Snufflekins. Melanie Blackwood. It is an honour."

Jem sensed rather than felt Mel tense at the mention of her name, but he was careful to keep his long perfected bored expression in place. No doubt the demon had many tricks up his sleeve and knowing their names was likely the least of them.

"Please." Var waved a hand wide, gesturing to the empty sofa that faced him. "Come join me and tell me what it is I can do for you today."

Mel hesitated, but Jem gave her a subtle nudge as he made his way over to the demon. *Get your game face on.*

At his silent words, she straightened and followed more confidently behind him – if only she was always so obedient. She stopped shy of the sofa, clearly realising that any attempt to scale the thing in her current size would undermine the confident persona she was trying to project. Jem debated floating her up for the fun of seeing her flail around and turn that funny red shade she got when she was annoyed with him, but decided that their purpose here was more important than amusing himself.

"We need a dragon heart stone," she told the demon, who looked down at her with an amused twinkle in his eye.

Var took a long sip of his drink as he considered this. "They are rare. What will you give me in return?"

Mel stiffened ever so slightly, no doubt counting how many minutes of her fragile human life she had to barter. "What do you want?"

Jem barely refrained from groaning and burying his head in his paws. What was she thinking, giving the demon free rein on the bidding? Had she learned nothing in their time in this stupid market?

There was a long silence as Var swished the liquid around in his glass. When he finally returned his attention to them, there was barely concealed eagerness in the silver eyes that now had an unworldly hue to them.

"A memory."

Jem hissed.

Mel looked between them, confusion scrunching her brow. "What?"

"I want a single memory from your past." Var gave Jem a wicked smile. "Both of your pasts."

"But, why –"

*Demons feed off human emotion,* Jem told her, an uncomfortable lump settling in his stomach.

Her mouth went slack in understanding. *You mean he wants us to relive something bad so he can feed off our emotion?*

*Yes.*

She turned to the demon, once more wary. "What kind of memory?"

"A memory of my choosing. It will cause you no physical harm, and your mind and memories will remain wholly intact."

He waved a hand, and the wall next to him shimmered. An oily patch appeared on its surface and spread out until it was roughly the size of a doorway – a weird, undulating doorway.

"What you seek is inside. You simply have to step through. In doing so, you will share with us one of your memories, then you will leave with your stone. Simple."

Mel gave Jem a questioning glance. The uncertainty in her eyes mirrored his own conflicted feelings. He wasn't stupid enough to believe there wasn't a catch to all this; the demon was being purposely vague. But they needed that damn stone.

Seeming unconcerned, Var relaxed back on the sofa. "Of course, you could always find another demon to supply the stone." He took a slow sip of his drink, watching them over the glass. "Though you may be hard-pressed to find any left in the market. I believe there was some ... disruption, and many of my brethren have vacated lest the situation draw the attention of the authorities." He smirked knowingly at them.

Jem silently cursed. That explained the exodus that seemed to be occurring as they'd made their way here. Could they find another demon, or was Var telling the truth? Even if they did, another demon might demand a higher price.

*It's your call*, he told Mel, already regretting the words as soon as they left his head.

"Fine," she said to the demon. Her mouth set into a grim line as she eyed the inky stain on the wall. "You swear it will do us no harm?"

"I do."

"And we just have to step through and retrieve the stone. There are no nasty surprises on the other side."

Var spread his arms wide. "It's as simple as that."

Mel's swallow was audible. She nodded and turned to Jem. "I'll go first."

He wasn't going to argue.

Squaring her shoulders, Mel stepped up to the shimmering doorway that rippled on the wall. She reached out a hand to touch it and hesitated. With a deep breath, she stepped forward. And was swallowed by the inky blackness.

The doorway pulsed and shuddered, then turned pearlescent. Jem rushed forward to see what had happened to Mel, only to skid to a stop when the milky surface changed once more.

An image appeared, slowly growing more distinct. A young girl with brown hair in cute pigtails. She carried a stuffed black cat in her arms, its fur ragged and an eye missing. The child – six years old, maybe seven – ran with a beaming smile to an older woman, a white page flapping in hands.

The blue eyes that turned to the child were the same colour as Mel's, and the woman's features were similar enough that Jem assumed her to be Mel's mother. But that was as far as the resemblance went. Where even as a child, Mel's blue eyes were bright with life and curiosity, there was a coldness to the older woman's that suggested empathy was little more than a word in the dictionary to her.

Young Mel tugged on the sleeve of her mother's crisp white blouse as she bounced up and down on her toes, a beaming smile on her face. "Look, Mommy. I drew Kitty Cat."

The woman frowned down at her daughter and carefully extricated her sleeve. "You are meant to be studying, Melanie, not drawing. How do you ever expect to get a place in the Coven if you don't work hard? Don't you want to be like your mother?"

The little girl's gaze shifted to the floor, but not before Jem caught the trembling of her lip or the crestfallen expression on her face.

"I was just playing familiars and... "

"No more excuses. Now, give me Kitty Cat."

An expectant hand was held out, and young Mel's eyes widened in horror. She hugged the stuffed cat closer to her, tears glistening in her eyes.

"I'll be good. I promise. I –"

Her mother snatched the cat from her grasp. "No more, Melanie. You're too old for such trivialities."

The image faded as the young child reached desperately for the stuffed animal that was held just out of her reach. In its place was a square white room, and in the centre, Mel stood with a single tear running down her cheek.

Var inhaled deeply, closing his eyes as he did so. "There's little more pure than the crushed dreams of childhood."

Jem hissed, his claws unsheathing with the urge to cut the demon. Only Mel's shaky voice stopped him from acting on the instinct.

"The stone is here, Jem." She took a shuddering breath, then reached for something out of his view. When she turned back, she held up a small black stone that seemed to glitter in her hand.

The demon turned that piercing gaze on him and smiled. "Your turn, familiar."

Jem stared as the doorway winked back to that ominous inky puddle, once more blocking Mel from his view. He could still see that small child though. The image was permanently imprinted in his mind, the pain on her face making his heart ache.

And something told him that was only the demon's warm-up act.

Slowly, Jem backed away from the undulating doorway. Screw this trip down memory lane; they'd find another demon and Mel would just have to give them her firstborn.

But Var wagged a finger at him. "The deal was for both of your memories, familiar. You are free to back out of the deal if you wish. But if you do, your witch will remain trapped inside forever."

# CHAPTER EIGHTEEN

J em froze. The demon's words hung in the air, the noose just waiting to tighten around his neck. He could leave, but then Mel would be trapped.

"Jem?" Mel called uncertainly from the unseen room beyond the oily doorway. "Is everything okay?"

Had she heard the demon's words? Her voice sounded wary but held no real fear.

As if aware of Jem's every thought, Var nodded. "She cannot hear us. She can only see or hear that which is in the white room with her."

Relief filled him, and the sensation was quickly followed by shame. He didn't want to leave her in there, but he could find another way to get her out. She wouldn't be trapped in there forever. And she'd never know what he'd done; he could tell her that the demon double crossed them.

He didn't have to relive his worst memories.

Even as he wanted desperately to cling to that thought, guilt settled over him like a grinding weight that refused to let him take even a step towards the exit.

Growling low in his throat, he gave the demon his dirtiest look, and stepped up to the oily smudge of a doorway. Whatever emotion this memory dragged from him, he hoped Var choked on it.

Second-guessing his life decisions, he stepped through. The shift was instant. Warmth washed over him, a feeling of utter contentment filling his chest until it seemed like he might burst. A gentle hand stroked his fur, tickled behind his ear. Her hand.

The familiar floral fragrance filled his nose with each slow inhale he took, and he felt safe in a way that he'd never felt before. He let her scent wrap around him, cocoon him in its embrace. This was what it was like to be loved.

"I need to talk to you, Jem."

At her sweet voice, he blinked his eyes open and looked up at her. There was a sadness in her green eyes, and he nuzzled into her, wanting to make it go away. He didn't want her to be sad.

"You've been with me a long time now. There's nothing more that I can teach you. You're ready to be a familiar."

Pride filled him at her words, at the confirmation that he'd done a good job for her. He wanted to be the best familiar for her. She deserved the best.

But instead of cuddling him closer and sharing in

his happiness, she looked away, her expression becoming distant.

"I'm sorry, Jem. It's time for you to go back to FFS so you can be assigned your forever witch."

He nudged her, confused. What did she mean? She was his forever witch.

She pulled her hand away, and the warmth leeched out of him, leaving a terrifying chill in its place. He reached out his paw for her, but she turned away, refusing to meet his questioning gaze.

The next face that appeared before him was not her kind, familiar face. It was that of a stone-faced witch aide. The next hands that held him were not her gentle, loving ones. They were the hard, uncaring hands of the man who came to bring him back to FFS.

The next witch he was assigned was not his forever witch. Because why would a witch ever want to keep him?

Jem blinked as the memory slowly faded. He was once again standing in the demon's office, and that floral fragrance was nothing but an echo of the past. The inky doorway was gone now, and Mel stood next to him with the dragon heart stone gripped tightly in her clenched fist. Fresh tears glistened in her eyes as she looked at him.

"Oh, Jem..."

For a moment, he stood there, paralysed by the aching sorrow that threatened to crush his chest. Then he shook himself, reaching out for the anger that had been his only true companion for all these years, and wrapped it around him as a shield against the pain. *Let's go.*

He turned and strode from the place without looking back. He didn't have to see the demon to know Var had gotten what he wanted. It was time they got out of this forsaken place.

Mel hurried to catch up with him. He could feel her concerned gaze burning into him, but he carefully avoided looking at her. Only when the demon's shop was out of view did he pause long enough for her to put the stone into his pack with the other ingredients.

Her hand lingered for a moment on his back after she closed the pack, her warmth seeping into him. The ache in his chest intensified.

"Well, well. Looky what we have here."

Jem snapped his head around and found the sorceress standing barely ten feet from them, flanked on either side by the leprechauns who had transported the phoenix. Rage twisted the woman's beautiful face into something savage and terrifying, and her hands were claws with nails extending like miniature knives from each finger.

He swore, cursing his stupidity. He should have been monitoring their surroundings for threats, not indulging in trips down memory lane and feeling sorry for himself.

Mel edged closer to him. She gripped his fur as tension radiated through their bond.

He assessed their options, knowing the odds of

them getting out of this in one piece were not good. *I'm going to distract them. You run.*

Her grip tightened. *Not without you.*

He risked taking his eyes away from the trio for only a fraction of a second, but it was enough for him to see the stubborn set of Mel's jaw. He sighed.

*Okay. You go over. I go under.*

*What do you mean ov –*

He didn't give her a chance to finish the question. He used his magic to pick her up and catapult her high over the head of the leprechaun on the left. As he did, he ran straight for the sorceress, taking the woman by surprise.

The woman screeched as he ran between her legs, swiping out with his claws and trying to trip her up. He added a couple of winding circles to disorientate the sorceress, then continued through to meet Mel on the other side as she landed.

*Run!* he ordered, urging Mel forward with a nudge of his head. She didn't need telling twice.

A sudden burst of energy from behind was the only warning he had before a rainbow speared the ground between them.

The ground exploded in a hail of colourful debris and they were thrown through the air. They landed with a thud on opposite sides of the path from each other, but he saw with relief that Mel was back on her feet and running in an instant.

He increased his speed, aiming for the small potions shack at the end of the row. Just inside the door, he could see shelves of colourful vials. He sent a burst of magic out to grab them and flung the vials over his head into the path behind him.

This time the sorceress was ready for his tricks, and she had her leprechaun bodyguard throw up a rainbow-coloured bubble around her. The potions smashed against it and dissolved into a harmless cloud of steam.

The leprechaun shot another rainbow spear in their direction. It forked, sending a stream of red light towards Jem, and blue light straight at Mel.

Jem rolled to the side, sending a burst of magic Mel's way as he did. He levitated her into the air right as the ground beneath her exploded. A crater remained where she'd been standing.

He shifted course, intending to rejoin her and make a swift dash for the exit. A hand closed around his tail, and he was yanked into the air.

The world turned upside down, and he found himself staring at a wide grin of golden teeth.

The second leprechaun.

Jem hissed and lashed out with his claws, but the leprechaun's long reach meant the strike connected only with air.

The leprechaun pulled a worn brown leather bag from a clip at his waist. He opened it with one hand and shoved Jem inside, snapping it closed.

All light disappeared.

Jem twisted and writhed, panic threatening to take hold as the bag tightened around him and the air was sucked away. He slashed with his claws, but the material didn't even fray. He reached for his magic. Nothing.

The place inside him where his magic usually resided felt empty and hollow. It was as if the leprechaun had taken a knife and carved out his very soul.

He struggled harder.

The bag jostled. Suddenly, light pierced the darkness, and Jem was airborne. His magic came flooding back to him.

In his moment of weightlessness, he dimly registered the stream of colourful swear words behind him. Then he hit the ground with a thud, and Mel was next to him.

"Run!" she yelled, not breaking stride.

Jem risked a glance back, knowing that split-second could cost him.

The leprechaun who had captured him lay in a heap on the ground, trying to untangle himself from a silver chain that appeared to have come from a nearby weapons shop and was now wrapped around his ankles.

Apparently, this had taken the sorceress and other leprechaun by surprise too, as they stumbled over their fallen ally in their hasty pursuit.

Jem turned his focus forward and raced after Mel. Together, they wove between the legs of exiting patrons and put as many obstacles as possible between them and their pursuers.

His heart pounded in his chest as the warehouse

entrance loomed before them. If they could make it out there, only the outer market and large metal archway would stand between them and freedom. Jem pushed his legs to move faster.

An opening appeared suddenly in the path before them as everyone abruptly moved to the side. Gasps of horror sounded as a robed figure stepped into the space.

*The* robed figure.

Jem skidded, attempting to halt his momentum, but he was going too fast. He slid to a stop – right at the figure's feet. With a sickening lurch of his stomach, he looked up into the cowl hood. Darkness stared back at him. And from within the darkness, two glowing green eyes met his.

"Mine."

The whispered word was a hiss on the wind and it wrapped around Jem, filling his veins with ice. He cowered back on his hind legs, choking on the terror that was clawing its way down his throat as he realised what the creature was. A wraith.

A desperate glance behind told him that the sorceress and her guards were closing the gap from that side, so they couldn't run back into the warehouse. There was no escape.

*What do we do?* Mel edged closer to his side, her gaze firmly fixed on the wraith that was apparently his new owner. She held her head high, but her hands trembled as she faced the terrifying creature.

*Don't suppose your coven studies taught you any offensive magic?*

Her grimace told him everything he needed to know.

The robed figure raised its right arm and pointed at Jem, a skeletal hand appearing from beneath the folds of cloth. The hand turned, and the wraith crooked a bony finger, beckoning him to come.

A wave of power settled over Jem, tightening like a physical bond around him. He dug his claws into the ground, scrabbling for purchase as something invisible pulled him forward.

It was fruitless. Try as he might to fight against it, the power was too strong. Inch by inch, the distance between him and those green eyes lessened.

Something jerked him to a stop.

An insistent tug came from the witch-familiar bond deep inside him. Belatedly, he registered Mel's urgent chanting. She was repeating the bonding ritual incantation over and over, holding tight to him through the bond's connection, even as the wraith's power sought to take control of him.

The two forces raged inside him, and Jem latched onto his connection to Mel for all he was worth. He joined her in frantically repeating the ritual words, over and over, embracing both the words and the intent behind them in a way he never had before.

The wraith's magic snapped like an elastic band, eliciting a piercing shriek of fury from within the darkness. The hand that had beckoned him forward clenched into a fist. It opened again and a shimmering red orb appeared, pulsating as it grew larger and larger.

The few patrons that remained nearby yelled in panic at the sight of the orb and dashed frantically for the metal archway.

Not one to miss a cue, Jem ran back to Mel's side. "Jump on," he ordered. He helped her up with a nudge of his magic.

A rainbow struck the ground next to them.

Jem swore.

Bounding into action, he turned and ran straight for the wraith and its strange pulsating ball. A burst of rainbow spears followed in his wake, sending earth spraying in all directions behind him.

The wraith's red orb vibrated and rose into the air above the skeletal hand. Magic crackled around it and the air became charged in warning.

Mel let out a shrill whistle, and Jem stumbled as the piercing sound sent pain shooting through his eardrum.

He was about to ask her exactly what she thought she was doing when a loud squawk answered her call. Jem jerked his head up in time to see the phoenix swoop down through the hole in the warehouse roof.

# CHAPTER NINETEEN

Phoenix fire blazed a trail behind them. Jem ran for all he was worth, the heat scorching his dark fur. He was dimly aware of the sorceress's screams as they faded in the distance, but he felt no sympathy for her; she deserved whatever she got.

The wraith and the leprechauns had all turned their attention to the flaming bird that seemed intent on burning them to a crisp. Their rainbow spears and strange red balls were having no effect on the creature, but bursts of colour continued to light up the sky as the metal structure of the warehouse groaned in protest under the onslaught.

Not many patrons had remained in the warehouse after the initial fire had triggered an exodus, but the few who had been brave enough to stick around now rethought their decision. Stallholders hurriedly packed up their most valuable items, abandoning the rest to the chaos, and shoppers all but trampled each other in their haste to escape.

Jem wove and dodged through the stampeding feet, the air around him crackling with the static charge of magic about to reach bursting point. Mel gripped his fur tightly, spurring him on as they made a beeline for the looming gates.

He spotted a familiar figure in the crowd ahead, and his vision narrowed.

The old battleaxe who had lured him to the underground auction shuffled with feigned frailty towards the exit. Her harmless mask was back in place, and even the market's hardened patrons were allowing the poor old lady space to move unhindered.

He'd seen the truth behind that mask, however. And he'd promised himself he'd make her pay before he left this place. Now was his chance.

Casting his eye around what remained of the outdoor stalls, he searched for something that would satisfy the burning need for revenge. The abandoned magical pranks stall caught his attention, and he grinned as he saw the pile of discarded objects lying by the wall next to it.

Sending out a tendril of magic, he grabbed a creepy doll that lay lifelessly on top of the pile and applied force to the soft spot at the centre of its chest. The doll's eyes flicked open and flashed red.

A wide grin split the plastic face, showcasing a terrifying set of jagged teeth. Slowly, the doll rose and looked around. With another nudge of magic, Jem floated it to the ground and aimed it at the old lady.

The doll lifted its arms, reaching for the woman. "Mama." With terrifying speed, it waddled after its target.

The old lady looked around in surprise and shrieked when she saw the creepy doll lumbering towards her with outstretched arms. She fumbled inside a pocket in her skirt and produced a purple potion that she flung at the offending toy.

The doll exploded into limb confetti.

Purple smoke filled the air as the doll's head thudded to the ground next to Jem. He ignored the still chomping teeth and scanned the near empty stalls for something else he could use.

His gaze fell on a sealed jar and his grin widened even further – enchanted flying bed bugs. Now, that's what he was talking about.

With a possibly overenthusiastic burst of magic, he sent the jar soaring through the air to smash at the old lady's feet. Glass shattered, and a black swarm rose into the air, surrounding the woman.

He watched with glee as she batted frantically at the insects, all pretence of being old and frail forgotten. She spun around in a bizarre dance routine that went from offensive avoidance to desperate scratching of every inch of exposed skin, and he savoured every second of her torment.

An urgent tug at his fur caused him to tense. Mel was no doubt going to berate him for being cruel to an old lady when they should be getting as far from here as possible.

But the lecture he expected didn't come. Instead, she gestured excitedly to a pile of rubbish that had been dumped two stalls down from the one with the bedbugs. It took him a moment to realise what she was pointing to, but when he did, she immediately shot up to the highest level of esteem he'd ever afforded a witch.

*Together?* she asked.

*Together.*

He let his magic reach out through the bond and twine with hers. As one, they gave an enthusiastic shove.

The glitter bombs exploded right as the old lady careened into the pile of rubbish. Silver and gold glitter burst into a cloud, obscuring her from view for a full minute. When the cloud finally settled, the woman was covered in so much sparkle that she looked like a cheap extra from Twilight.

There was nothing magically enhanced about the glitter to make her torture worse, but really there didn't need to be. The glitter would be an absolute bitch to get off. She'd be picking his revenge out of her nose hairs for weeks.

Satisfaction wrapped around him like a warm hug, and Mel gave a triumphant "whoop" as she clung tightly to his fur. He set his sights on the metal archway, and without sparing the old battleaxe another thought, he got them the hell out of the black market.

The shift was instantaneous. It was as if somebody simply flicked a switch and turned off the chaos that had been raging behind them. The yells and explosions were replaced by the distant hum of traffic and a blissful sense of peace.

It was almost as if they'd never even stepped foot in the market.

But they had, and night had fallen while they were there. The moon hung high overhead now, and while the rain had stopped, there was still a bitter chill to the air.

Mel gave a little shiver as she climbed down off his back. "Guess my warming tonic is wearing off." She gave a rueful smile. "The adrenaline must have made it burn off quicker than normal."

Jem looked up at the darkened sky, and a sliver of unease ran through him. "We were at the market for longer than we intended. We should get back before the inspector wakes up."

Mel scratched him behind the ear, and an involuntary purr rumbled low in his chest. She smiled. "Let's go."

Despite the absolute shit show the day had turned out to be, it seemed luck was on their side for the journey back. A bus pulled up minutes after they arrived – thankfully unhindered – at the bus stop. They slipped on, hidden between a group of workers too tired from a long day to notice the cat and miniature human at their feet.

As they huddled beneath one of the seats and tried

not to attract attention to themselves, Mel turned to him. *We make a pretty good team when we're not fighting with each other.*

Jem gave a mental *humph,* but at her chastising look, he acquiesced. *I guess so.*

*Can I ask you something?*

He tensed. No doubt she was going to press him about the memory that damn demon had forced from him. It was the last thing he wanted to talk about – especially not while he was still feeling raw from reliving the worst moment of his life.

*Why don't you like Derek?*

Jem blinked in surprise. Derek? Who was Derek?

It took a minute before he realised she was talking about the idiot she called her boyfriend.

*The douchebag? Because he's as fake as those teeth he's trying to pass off as his own. Besides, being mean to animals is the first warning sign of a serial killer.*

She rolled her eyes. *You didn't exactly paint yourself in the best light when you two met.*

*I was just having a bit of harmless fun. And you didn't see the way he acted when you left the room. That nice guy persona is all an act.*

*He's never been anything other than kind and thoughtful to me. Maybe you caught him on an off day?*

Jem didn't miss the flash of doubt that passed over her face. He shrugged, too tired to try make her see sense. He simply said, *You deserve better,* and rested his head down on his paws.

She raised her eyebrows at his assessment, but said

nothing, just lapsed into silence, seeming lost in her own thoughts. Jem really hoped those thoughts included imaginative ways to dump knobhead boyfriends, though he didn't hold out much hope. Humans were dumb.

As the adrenaline rush from escaping the market a free cat faded, he found his eyelids growing heavy. The vibration of the bus lulled him into a boneless state of relaxation, and thoughts of his warm bed danced tantalisingly before his eyes.

Mel turned to him suddenly, jolting him out of his doze. *Do you mind if we make a quick detour? It'll only take a few minutes.*

He gave a wide yawn and shrugged. He was far too tired to think right now.

When the bus screeched to a halt at the next stop, Mel ushered him towards the door. There were surprised yelps from several passengers as they hurried down the aisle, but they made it outside and onto the pavement with minimal drama.

The bus stop Mel had chosen was next to a quiet housing estate. He had no idea where they were – these places all looked the same to him – but he dutifully padded after Mel as she led him to the end of a cul-de-sac of identical white houses.

"What are we –"

She turned and frantically gestured for him to be quiet. Without a word, she ducked down behind a pristinely manicured hedge that ran along the path where they stood.

He gaped at her, wondering if she'd lost her mind. Then the front door of the house next to them swung open. Mel peered around the hedge, and he followed her line of sight.

A man and woman emerged from the house. The woman giggled at something her companion said and wrapped her arms around his waist. As he leaned down to oblige her with a kiss, the light from the hallway behind illuminated his features.

Douchebag Derek.

Mel watched the overly affectionate display with little more than a tightening of her jaw. When the two finally closed the door and disappeared down the road, she loosed a breath. "Guess you were right about him."

Jem tilted his head, curiosity narrowly outweighing his desire to slice the man up into little pieces for putting that look in her eyes. "Why did you want to come here?"

She shrugged, looking a little sheepish all of a sudden. "What you said bothered me. I wanted to see what he was like when he didn't know I was looking. I guess I thought you could float me up so I could peek in a window or something."

"I still can if you want?"

She gave a wry laugh. "I think I've seen enough, thanks." The humour leeched from her face as she dropped her gaze to the ground. "I can't believe my mother would set me up with such a dick."

"Your mother set you up –" Jem shook his head. "Never mind. You're better off without him."

Mel nodded but didn't meet his eyes, and the urge to put his claws to good use reared its head once more.

"Want to get a little revenge?" he asked.

At the sly suggestion, she turned to him. Her expression was still shuttered, but he didn't miss the gleam of interest caught by the moonlight.

"What have you got in mind?"

# CHAPTER TWENTY

They were still laughing by the time they reached Mel's house half an hour later. Derek's door had had no magical enchantments to prevent Jem from using his lock-picking skills, and they'd easily slipped into the house. Unfortunately, Mel had vetoed his idea to lie in wait and kill Derek in his sleep – apparently that was too extreme a punishment for the human. They had, however, left a few surprises for the douchebag.

Jem was just picturing Derek's face when he climbed into bed that night as the door to the house flung open to reveal a frantic Elena.

"Oh, thank Hecate you're back. He's waking up."

His stomach dropped as next to him, Mel tensed. They'd gotten so caught up in their little revenge plot that they'd completely forgotten about the ticking time bomb that was unconscious in Mel's living room.

Together, the three of them hurried into the house.

The inspector lay on the sofa where they'd left him earlier that day, and the magical chain still bound him. He stirred, and though his eyes hadn't yet opened, it was clear from his jerky movements that he was becoming aware of the chain's restriction.

"Jem," Mel whispered, barely contained urgency edging her voice. "Get the chains off him."

He eyed the man who seemed to grow more agitated in his half-conscious state. It would be much easier to kill the inspector and dispose of the body if they kept him restrained.

Mel nudged him with a frown, and he sighed. Against his better judgement, he focused his magic on the chain. It obeyed his order and unravelled from the man, sliding harmlessly from the sofa to land in a neat pile on the floor. As it hit the ground, Ciaran's eyes snapped open and he jerked upright.

He darted panicked glances around the room. "What happened? Where am I?"

Elena hurried to his side, wringing her hands together. "Are you okay? You fell and bumped your head and –"

"It's okay, Elena." Mel stepped up next to her friend and placed a calming hand on her leg.

Jem hissed. What in the name of Hecate was she doing? The inspector could see her.

Ciaran blinked a couple of times and frowned in confusion. He looked from Mel to Elena and back again.

"Melanie Blackwood, I assume?"

Mel nodded. "Inspector –"

"Ciaran. Please."

She nodded in acknowledgement. "Ciaran. I must apologise. As you can see" – she indicated to herself – "there's been a slight mishap."

He raised an eyebrow, but his expression gave nothing away as he waited silently for her to continue.

"I was concerned about looking bad in front of FFS, so I asked my friend here to assist with the inspection. As you can probably gather, things didn't quite go according to plan."

The inspector looked down at himself and at the chain now resting on the floor. His lips quirked with what looked like amusement. "You don't say."

Mel's cheeks reddened and she squirmed. "Yeah, about that –"

"It was my fault," Elena jumped in. "I didn't mean to knock you out, honestly. We just thought that if Jem and Mel could get the ingredients they needed from the black market, we could fix it all, and then Jem wouldn't be in trouble and..."

The room fell silent as everybody gaped at her in disbelief. Jem groaned and sank to the floor. If he hadn't already been screwed, he most definitely was now.

Seeming to realise she'd put her foot in it, Elena withered, cowering into herself. She cast an apologetic look down at Mel.

Ciaran scrubbed a hand over his face and blew out

a long breath. "Okay. First things first." He turned to look at Mel, giving her a tired smile. "I'm assuming you'd prefer not to remain this size. Do you have what you need to fix it?"

She nodded silently, no doubt afraid to say anything else and add more fuel to the fire after Elena's outburst.

"Let's get that sorted. Then I think we all need to have a long talk."

Jem stared at the man, confused. The inspector was far too calm for somebody who'd just found out they'd tried to trick him before magically roofieing him. No doubt he was lulling them into a false sense of security before he brought the hammer down on them.

Warily, Jem followed behind as Mel led Ciaran upstairs. Elena opted to stay downstairs and tidy up in the kitchen. He wasn't sure there was actually anything that needed tidying up, but her wide-eyed panic told him it was probably best she stay far away from any sort of magic preparations right now.

"May I?" Ciaran asked, offering Mel his hand as they reached the ladder to the attic.

She gave him a grateful smile, and he carefully helped her up the steps and into the room above them.

Jem snorted as he followed. He could have floated her up.

Ciaran let a low whistle as he took in Mel's potion room, which was perfectly illuminated by the cool light of the moon. "Nice space you have here. Did you do the pentagram yourself?"

Mel smiled shyly at the compliment. "I've been working on it for a long time."

"It's very impressive."

Jem puked a little in his mouth as he watched the exchange. Why was the inspector being so nice to her? Obviously, he'd decided Mel had been led astray by the wicked familiar and was buttering her up so they could all gang up on Jem when the time came. Yep, that had to be it.

"So, what can I do to help?" Ciaran asked, taking in the large oak table and rows of jars containing potion ingredients.

Mel looked up at the table to the purple notebook that rested there. "The reversal spell is in my notebook. If you could help me up, I can –"

Before she could finish her sentence, Jem sent a cushion of air out with his magic and floated her gently up to rest on the table next to the notebook. The inspector wasn't the only one who could be helpful.

He leapt up to land beside her and met Ciaran's amused look with a blank stare.

Mel gave him a quick scratch behind the ear, her blue eyes twinkling. "Thanks, Jem."

She turned her attention to the notebook and flicked to a page that contained a list of ingredients carefully written out in her neat handwriting. As she scanned it, she reached over and undid the pack from his back.

Without removing the three restricted ingredients, she turned the notebook around so that it was facing

Ciaran. "Could you get me these ingredients from the shelf, please?"

The inspector looked over the list for a moment, then nodded and set about efficiently gathering the required jars and stacking them in an orderly row on the table where Mel could reach them.

Mel got to work preparing the reversal potion, pausing occasionally when her size required her to ask for help from either Jem or Ciaran. Within fifteen minutes, she had a thick blue concoction bubbling away in a small black cauldron. Only then did she open the small pack and carefully remove the three ingredients they'd gotten at the market.

Ciaran looked at them with wide-eyed surprise, but said nothing.

Jem held his breath as she added first the belladonna, then what remained of the phoenix feather, and finally the dragon heart stone to the mixture. What if it didn't work? What if, after all they'd been through, Mel was stuck this size? Guilt and worry twisted his insides, and he felt suddenly nauseated.

The mixture fizzled for a moment, a bubblegum scent filling the room. Mel switched off the heat beneath the cauldron. She swallowed nervously as she stared at the potion. "Guess this is it."

At her request, Ciaran helped her pour the liquid into a small vial so it was easier for her to consume. She screwed her face up and knocked it back in one go.

A minute passed and nothing happened.

Jem sank to the table, a horrible numbness settling over him. This was all his fault. If he hadn't –

Mel gasped.

The air filled with static, and suddenly, she started to grow. She stared in awe as first, her hand grew bigger, then her arms lengthened, followed by her legs. It was the most bizarre thing Jem had ever seen and he couldn't help his shocked laughter as he watched her, bit by bit, return to her normal size.

Within minutes, a fully grown Mel was sitting on the table next to him, tears of laughter running down her cheeks. "Well, that was interesting."

And that was enough to set Jem off again. His relief, coupled with exhaustion from a crazy day, sent him into a hysterical giggling fit that only caused Mel to laugh even harder. For a long time, the two lay there, unable to catch their breath as they clutched their sides.

Eventually, they were spent, and reality came crashing down on Jem once more. He sat up to find Ciaran watching him and Mel with an odd expression on his face. All remaining traces of humour left him.

"I think it's time we had that chat," Ciaran told them.

Together, they returned downstairs to join Elena in the kitchen. Mel made them all tea – which Jem noted Ciaran left untouched, clearly afraid of being drugged – and they sat around the island to answer the inspector's questions.

Jem didn't reach out telepathically to Mel to get

163

their stories straight. She'd already put enough on the line for him; he wouldn't ask anything more of her. Instead, he sat quietly with his eyes downcast as she recounted everything from the potion spilling to their foray in the dark market.

When she'd finished, there was a long drawn-out silence.

Jem lifted his head, ready to face the condemnation that was no doubt waiting for him, and found the inspector looking at him thoughtfully. The man's expression gave away nothing of what he was thinking, and Jem squirmed uneasily.

"Jem," Ciaran said. "Do you mind if I speak with Mel in private?"

Jem looked at Mel and she gave him a reassuring smile, but his stomach dropped. This was it. She was going to turn him in to FFS. She had no choice, not now the game was up.

Without a word, he jumped down off the counter and padded out of the kitchen. Maybe they'd at least let him have one last sleep in his bed with Mr. Fluffles before they took him away?

Feeling strangely heavy, he made his way up to his room. No, not his room. Not for much longer anyway. Something like regret settled over him as grabbed the stuffed bunny and curled up on the soft bed, hugging it close.

He drifted into a restless sleep. Flashes of the black market came to him, amplified in the way that only dreams could. The wraith's chilling green eyes as it reached for him. The blazing heat of flame ready to devour Mel and him unable to reach her. The demon's cackling laugh as he replayed Jem's most painful memory over and over again. When the sound of voices from downstairs snapped him awake, he was almost grateful.

Climbing reluctantly out of bed, he moved to the bedroom door. He'd left it open when he'd come upstairs, too weary to bother closing it. As a result, he could hear Mel and the inspector speaking quietly at the front door. He padded to the edge of the stairs and peered down.

Mel stood at the open door, unaware of him watching as she faced out into the night. She held out a white envelope to Ciaran.

"You'll give this to the Elders for me?"

Ciaran took hold of the letter but didn't take it from her. He tilted his head and smiled. "You owe me dinner if I do this."

She gave a low laugh. "I'll owe you two. Just get it to them quickly. I don't want to draw this out any longer than necessary."

With that, the inspector put the envelope on top of his clipboard and bid her farewell.

Sorrow sent a painfully familiar ache through Jem's chest and he sank to the floor. He wasn't surprised that she was turning him in – it was to be expected, really. But after everything they'd been through, the fact she sounded so eager to be rid of him was the bit that hurt most.

# CHAPTER TWENTY-ONE

Jem stood once more in front of the FFS Disciplinary Council. Thirteen pairs of eyes stared down at him from the gilded cushions on the raised dais, his mother at the centre. The chamber felt colder than usual, harsher. More unforgiving.

He hadn't been surprised when the summons had come early that morning. Still, he couldn't deny the sting of hurt at having his suspicions confirmed – Mel had asked to be rid of him as quickly as possible.

At least he'd gotten to have some fun before FFS stripped his powers. Not too many familiars could boast being responsible for the black market burning down. That was a pretty good way to go out with a bang.

"Jeremiah Snufflekins," Magdalena began, drawing the room to a hush. "We hadn't expected to see you again quite so soon. To say it is a surprise would be an understatement."

There was no emotion in her voice, but he was too tired to feel annoyed about her lack of maternal empathy. She'd made it clear last time that their genetic relationship would come second to her duty to FFS. Maybe if she'd ever been a proper mother to him, he'd have been more emotionally capable of bonding with a witch. Maybe he wouldn't have been so unlovable.

"We received a request from your assigned witch," Magdalena continued. "Melanie Blackwood has put forward a petition for you to be her Furever Familiar."

Jem jerked his head up, sure he must have misheard.

"Given your track record and the fact this decision requires agreement from both parties, we felt it was important to bring you here and put the choice to you."

His head was spinning so much that what she was saying didn't quite make sense. He recognised the words, of course, understood what she was asking him, but his brain was still waiting for the declaration that his magic was to be stripped. Not for a second had he expected ... this.

A seed of hope flared to life in his chest, a seed that he'd believed long buried. As soon as he recognised it, fear gripped him. Fear that the hope would be taken away again.

"Do you need time to consider your answer?" The question was asked softly, a gentleness creeping into his mother's voice that was rarely there.

He looked up at her, his voice cracking as he asked, "She wants me to stay?"

Magdalena inclined her head. "She does. Her petition states that she has reviewed her previously chosen path of the covens and no longer believes it to be the right one for her. While she acknowledges that you are contrary and difficult to reason with, she also states that you have shown courage and loyalty, and she feels the bond that has developed between you is a precious gift not to be squandered."

For the first time in his long life, Jem didn't know what to say. He'd come here expecting to lose everything. Never once had he hoped –

"Jem?"

He jerked around at the sound of Mel's voice. She stood at the entrance to the FFS chambers, Ciaran at her side. Her hands were clasped tightly in front of her as if she was trying not to fidget, and her blue eyes were watching him, uncertain.

"You don't have to say yes if you don't want to. The Council have agreed to sign off on your rehabilitation even if you say no. They will find another assignment for you – one that doesn't involve a witch bond. If that's what you want."

She was giving him an out? She was giving him a chance to be left alone, no pressure to form an unbreakable bond with someone who would inevitably let him down. Or...

He swallowed down the fear. He wouldn't let it rule him – not anymore.

*How would you ever find a decent boyfriend if I wasn't there to save you from your terrible taste in men?* He looked pointedly at Ciaran.

A grin split her face at his silent words. "Does that mean...?"

Jem turned to face the Elders. "I accept."

Mel screeched and launched herself at him from the doorway. She enveloped him in her arms and proceeded to kiss him all over.

"Ew, get off me, human." He swatted at her with his paw, but he didn't really put up much of a fight. Instead, he nuzzled into her, relishing the warmth of her embrace.

She was his witch. His forever.

And he was about to turn her life upside down. The least he could do was let her have her moment.

With a contented purr, he snuggled in closer. *Can we go home now?*

# AUTHOR NOTE

Thank you for joining me on this fun new adventure. I'm pretty sure I had more fun writing Jem's character than any other to date (maybe too much :) . This book has been a bit of a passion project, but there will definitely be more to come from the characters in the future.

If you enjoyed this book, I would be very grateful if you could leave a brief review (it can be as short as you like) on the site where you purchased your copy. As an author, reviews are the most powerful tools in my arsenal when it comes to finding new readers, and Jam promises to put you on the "do not shrink" list.

## ALSO BY L.M. HATCHELL

In the interest of saving (what's left of) my sanity, I've decided to direct all updates for my books to my website. This will be the most up to date list and guarantee you won't miss anything due to me forgetting to update old files.

So, if you want to find out more about my other books and series, please visit:

https://lmhatchell.com/books

Milton Keynes UK
Ingram Content Group UK Ltd.
UKHW011447050524
442175UK00004B/158